Where We Dwell
Pangyrus 10

For information about permission to reproduce selections from this book,
please write to Permissions at info@pangyrus.com

Cover art thanks to Miranda Loud. You can find more of her work at
mirandaloudartist.com.
Composition by Esther Weeks
Print Production Manager: Kayla Griffin

Founding Editor: Greg Harris
Managing Editor: Amanda Lewis
Asst. Managing Editor: Yelena Chzhen
Fiction Editors: Anne Bernays, Virginia Pye
Assoc. Fiction Editor: Otis Fuqua
Poetry Editor: Cheryl Clark Vermeulen
Assoc. Poetry Editor: Cynthia Bargar
Nonfiction Editor: Artress White
Assoc. Nonfiction Editor: Molly Howes
Zest! Editor: Deborah Norkin
Schooled Editors: Christelle Saintis, Michaela Gaziano
In Sickness & In Health Editor: Amy Glynn
Field Notes Editor: Rachel West
Reviews Editor: Anri Wheeler
Columns Editor: Apratim Gautam
Generations Editor: Aime Card
Editorial Assistants: Eliza Greenbaum and Virginia Clarke

Pangyrus
2592 Massachusetts Ave #2
Cambridge, MA 02140
pangyrus.com

Contents

Note from the Editor

Trees, biologists tell us, don't exist. Not in the way scientists prefer things exist, with lines separating the categories and a shared genetic ancestry.

A famous zen parable might illustrate. A man fleeing an enraged tiger finds himself trapped against a precipitous drop, and goes over the cliff edge to escape. The low shrubby bush that he crashes through to reach the cliff? A mix of stunted fir and black spruce, neither plant reaching, in that place of whistling winds and cold exposure, even as high as the stinging nettles that score his shins with venom.

He saves himself by grabbing the wooden elbow of a bittersweet, the vine thick enough to sustain his weight, its bark tough as an old oak's.

Suspended there between earth and sky, with death baring its teeth above him and sharp rocks threatening below, what can he do? He sees a delicate dark green plant growing on the rockface and, nestled within, a perfectly ripe red strawberry. He plucks it with his free hand and eats. *Ahh*, he thinks. *Delicious.*

Two plants in this story share a common genetic ancestor that is a tree: the strawberry and the nettle.

Harrumphs Andrew Groover, of the USDA's Institute for Forest Genetics, in a 2005 article: "Forest trees constitute a contrived group of plants that have more in common with herbaceous relatives than we foresters like to admit."

"Dwelling," as a concept, has much in common with the category "tree." We seem to see and experience it — we can point to places we've definitely lived — and yet when we broaden our view across time and circumstance, the stability and durability implied in the term disintegrates into an artifact of memory, a trick of perspective. The course of our life will be full of dwellingplaces — and yet in none of them do we fully dwell. The form of our life is desire and movement, the pattern of our days set by "good enough for nows" and "get to it laters" and "thank God for thats."

We exist in tension, forever craving something that abides, and forever evolving, losing, outgrowing, moving through. The moments of peace, where time appears in an endless present, are visible mainly in retrospect, with the passage of memory's smoothing thumb over what was in actuality a perpetually stormy brow, an anxiousness that never came to rest while we were actually doing the living.

And the equilibrium we attribute to others? Even if we've been lucky enough to have a stable childhood, our parents change. These fixed, eternal gods, whose decreed routines set our foundations, descend from the clouds, reveal themselves as mortals no more adult than we are: going flat out, juggling the next set of bills, dozing off at meetings, exhausted by deadlines and indecision, with a catalog of problems whose solutions, year by year, grow more elusive. We may have inherited the fantasy, born of imperialism and colonialism, that out there are humans whose lives are harmonious, natural, sustainable. It's marketing. Condescension. Spend some time anywhere. People will tell you. We're day to day.

Pangyrus 10 marks a milestone on the way to an anniversary. It's our 10th print anthology, arriving a year before our 10th year in existence. On the one hand, it seems too small a number: if we publish two volumes a year, how is this just the 10th? On the other, it seems like an improbable achievement, given the butterfly lifespan of literary magazines. The answer to the apparent conundrum is the same in both instances: this is our 10th anthology because we keep adapting and growing. Alongside anthologies like this one, full of unexpected connections and ranging across genres, we're publishing chapbooks like *What Tells You Ripeness* and focused collections that are effectively books, like *Next: Visions Toward a Less-Divided America*. We're publishing a steady 2-3 pieces a week online. It's a powerful formula we've improvised our way towards day to day, as we reach both new and sustaining readers with the work of an ever-more-expansive community of contributors.

This anthology sprang from discussions during the heart of the pandemic shutdowns, when we were far too stuck in our dwellingplaces — and at the same time, for some of us, more outdoors in our local neighborhoods and parks than we'd ever been before. Turkeys, goats, coyotes, skunks, and even bears were stirring into the quiet spaces left by our absence. The air — cleared. This temporary effect of one natural crisis on the ongoing, larger environmental chaos and emergency of climate change was a reminder that the feeling of the world ending is just that — a feeling. The world is always also beginning. And neither beginnings nor endings conform to our expectations, we who live, as we must, in the eternal middle between fears and hopes. Here between earth and sky, we look for pleasure, insight, a taste of the gift we're offered only in the present.

This anthology is full of such gifts, from the resurrection in moss of Andrea Cohen's opening poem "Coming Back," to the apocalyptic but accepting closing wish in Michael Walsh's "Kinship of Smoke and Flow":

> …Waterways, take
> and remake our ashes in your deeps.

The theme in so many works in this volume is evolution, transformation. A lost relationship is continually renewed by visitations in Nancy Huggett's "A Birder's Eye." Rebecca Watkins, in "Hiking Boots," claims the power of her own body and judgment out on the trails. Sudden, even shocking ends — the aura of death that suffuses Beto Caradepiedra's short story

"Jaguar" — are revealed more as shifts in a balance. Nowhere is this more beautifully, and tragically, figured than in the somber way "Lobo" hands over responsibility from a fallen activist to us, the living: "You guard the forest."

Other pieces reclaim our relationship to place, the particularities of time and light and sense that make up memory and identity. There is the lightning-flash immanence of Pamela Wax's "The Mighty Mississippi" where

> ...truth cracks, redounding in glass panes,
> floorboards, and our bones

There is the distance of Judy Bolton-Fasman's "El Rincón de Recuerdo," the corner of memory that holds, not her mother's childhood in Cuba, nor even the photographs of her mother's childhood in Cuba, but the haunting effects of memory playing over everything that is lost without ever going away. The sense, beneath the overreactions of Scott Gould's "Playing Chicken," that as a known place changes and becomes other, so too does the self — in both challenging and revealing ways.

We dwell not alone but with others — and in these pages is an enduring fascination with our human relationships to the animal and natural world, from the love of one adoptee for another in Sarah Baldwin's "Held," to the near-impossible parental labor of nurturing young creatures through adolescence in Diana Renn's "Fledged." In Kelly Hevel's "An Absence in the Air," human life is changed when a non-human giant is felled; in DeMisty D. Bellinger's "Surfeit," the mourning is palpable for "a mistreated earth/ growing between our toes."

Then there's the test, the trying, the life we live in an attempt to stay whole for a time. In Spencer Brown's "Bloodlines," ghosts walk "under the canopy of cedars and pines," remnants of a "life we burned up before we ever knew we had it." In Taylor Sprague's "In Defense of Trans Childhood" no less than in Karen Paul's "Somatic Code," the body, to use Bessel Van Der Kolk's phrase, keeps the score. And in CB Anderson's "Man and Sky in Daytime," an astonishing, precise evocation of the relationship between Renee and Georgette Magritte, we see the movement — desperate, inspired, only minimally predictable by consciousness — between lived reality and art, between the seen and unseen, the vulnerable and triumphant.

Where we dwell, we need the shelter of each other.

On that note: A hearty thank you to the many people whose editorial and production work contributed to this volume: Managing Editor Amanda Lewis and Assistant Managing Editor Yelena Chzhen worked tirelessly across continents on editing and selection with our editors of Fiction, Nonfiction, and Poetry. Designer Esther Weeks and our new Print Production Manager Kayla Griffin wrangled the text into the shape you find it here. Miranda Loud graciously lent us permission to use her artwork on the cover, and together with Doug Woodhouse, our longtime cover designer, made us look fantastic.

And of course we owe our thanks to you, our readers. Chased as we are by the fearsome bills coming due of time and money, you are our grip on existence. Glad to be here with you, plucking this fine strawberry from the tree.

Greg Harris
Cambridge, Massachusetts

Coming Back

by Andrea Cohen

for Jane Mead

I'd want to be
moss, she said —

moss, which greens
where grass can't —

a softness, a carpet
that doesn't fly

off, which isn't
magical, but

simply is
where

she isn't.

A Birder's Eye

by Nancy Huggett

Out birding together, my mother and I would drop into a silent, side-by-side communion of awe, amazed that the world could reward this simple stillness with swift sightings of feathered creatures. We shared a certain sense of quiet excitement and frustration at our combined inability to master key identifiers. Accidental birders, neither of us kept a life list. Instead, we made smaller checklists and notations forgotten in birding books, novels, travel books, night table drawers. We chanted mantras of field marks that would distinguish Bonaparte from black-headed gull, piping from semipalmated plover. Always muttering markers and silhouettes as we rushed back from our walk, we would later find that the bird we were certain we had spotted could only be found, according to *Sibley's Guide to Birds*, in some small corner of Texas, not here on the southern coast of Maine, or at the top of the mountain in Montreal — wherever we happened to be wandering that day.

Red-Tailed Hawk

I am driving trance-like along the Trans-Canada Highway after the whirlwind downward spiral of Mum's cancer diagnosis, funeral, and the purging of her two-room apartment. The sudden loss and energy vortex has left me empty of anything but tears and tiredness. Then, somewhere in the flat tree-lined wasteland past Rigaud, I spot a ragged red-tailed hawk sitting forlorn, slightly worse for wear, in a barren October tree. As I rush toward it, it stares at me, stares at the red Subaru — the one my brother mocked me for buying, him not knowing that it would allow the hawk to spot me. I feel its eyes on the red car, on me driving the red car, watching me, turning its head as I pass by. This tattered hawk that makes me shiver and cry with delight, all at once. It's a certain intimation that Mum is here, my mother here, moulting her cancer-battered body, just one last glance as I glide by to let me know that she is shedding her earth-bound being, but is present, watching, here watching.

Was she watching? Would she watch? She let me go so easily. That was our way. A leaving and a coming together, a leaving and a coming together and never having to worry about the connection. There was no wish on my part for proof of her love, her approval. Only a recognition, cellular perhaps, of our birthing tie, the genes that held us and that she fostered (then let me go), fostered, then let me go. I was, in many ways, an easy child. The easy child making difficult choices — to leave the confines of privilege, to write, to birth before marriage — but still an easy child. And we braided our lives, if not with lifestyle, with interests and adventures that kept bringing us back together, that fed the deep stream of meaning that became the wellspring of my being. A sense of wonder and connection to something bigger, born in her little-girl self in the silent wilderness of northern Quebec, and shared with me at the ocean's edge in Maine, or under the expansive sky in Saskatchewan. She slyly inculcated a love for things that could not be measured in my father's accounting ledgers, encounters that held a deeper, more mysterious, and unexpected beauty. Poetry, prairies, prayer, birds.

Northern Harrier
For my 60th birthday, my husband gifts me a week with friends at Goose Rocks Beach in our traditional family rental right on the ocean. Women friends. Just a crones' week at the emptying beach in the shortening days of autumn. A long-awaited respite from caregiving, among women who care for me just by being present to the sunrise and the sunset and the long stretch of fine sand and seaweed that calls for lengthy walks at low and high and all the tides between. The glowing amber evening light from the cottage holds warmth and wine and melding of music that blends all our diverse stories. The gentle rhythm of the days soothes my bereft soul with sighs of surrendering and just breathing. Then, early one morning, meditating on the flat granite rock perched on the edge overlooking the

expanse of beach, ocean, sky, I feel a swoosh of air that lands on the jutting rock beside me. I open my eyes and slowly turn and look straight into the lemon eyes of a harrier hawk, one rock over. I hold my breath, my mantra gone. Stare into harrier eyes, harrier eyes into mine. I whisper "Mum." It crooks its head, then pushes off the rock and I can feel the whoosh and rush of air as it swoops back over the marsh behind us.

We learned to carry a bird book with us, Mum and me, and to travel with birders. In Maine, as soon as we arrived at the beach, we would go to the corner store, perched precariously on the edge of the marsh just behind our ocean-front cottage, and pick up the tourist news where the weekly bird walks and Audubon talks were posted, and we would plan our days around them. Up early just before the sun, we learned to drive to the back end of the golf course and wind our way through the weeds and the meadow on the cliff to the narrow walkway around the point to the north end of Biddeford Pool. Early, with thermos, binoculars, and bird book, we'd sit still, waiting for the sun and the birds to rise. This, a break from the hours of just sitting in our low beach chairs, saying nothing, or nothing much, or something so deep and personal it was as if we had whispered each other's longings into the sea wind.

A Riot of Birds

At home, after a particularly fractious morning with my daughter, who is recovering from a brain injury that causes unpredictable spurts of anger and aggression, I retreat to the living room and sit on the couch to mask my tears and look out the window, somewhere away from the confines of this house, my life. It is February, not yet spring. February, not really a bird month. Suddenly chaos erupts in the leafless maple out front. A riot of flitting birds. A pair of cardinals, a blue jay, a wren, a junco, a woodpecker, the tree all in turmoil. A distraction, a comfort. It's Mum out there, still Mum out there, making me laugh. I am with you, with you, with you, she calls. I wipe my tears and keep mothering. Mothering.

In her later years, my mother's unique solution to our challenge of identification was to have me accompany her on wild adventures to far-flung isles — the Galapagos, the Faroes, Norwegian fjords — where the birds were difficult to mistake, especially under the gentle tutelage of trained ornithologists. They travelled with us, along with geologists, oceanographers, and even a poet or two, on small expedition boats and pangas as we walked among blue-footed boobies, kayaked with puffins, or climbed tall cliffs under the diving and deadly zip-line plunge of the great skuas. They all fell in love with her calm curiosity and were happy to follow her from panga to whale spotting deck to smoking room, carrying her coffee, her binoculars, her small knapsack. She attracted scientists, artists, and kitchen staff with her quiet questions and intensely respectful and inquiring eyes, then retreated to her knitting as she and I reviewed the days and the sightings. She said she loved my eagerness for adventure, my enthusiasm for every new sighting — common or rare. She forgot this was her teaching, her gift to me. Schooled by random car trips to the outskirts of the city where she would gently prompt, hands ready on the steering wheel: now which way? Leaving direction up to me. I learned the fun was in the dead ends, the detours — the misread map, the sudden apparition of pottery studio, shed, farmer's field — not the final destination.

Sandhill Crane

The first thing I do when I arrive in Florida, is buy a bike. A cheapish Walmart cruiser. The beach is steep in Tequesta and walks at high tide can only take you so far. So, for breaks in helping my brother sort through and pack up my mother's beach condo, small respites from the forced confrontation with memory and a life, I ride. My brother John has dealt with his portion — golf paraphernalia, cookery, linen. He leaves the clothes, books, and AA medallions to me. We ride everyday before dinner, the same paths along the coast, until I convince him to throw the bikes in the back of the car and drive us to Jonathan Dickinson State Park inland on the nearby Loxahatchee. We unload and follow the narrow flat trails in and out of pine scrub, flatwood, wet prairie, dome swamps, meandering river, moss covered trees. At the first turn, just before the wooden bridge I jolt on the brakes, almost causing John to backend me. There, crossing the stream beside the wooden bridge and oblivious to bikers, is a Sandhill crane, red-crowned, tall and tawny, nudging a scattering of chicks across the shallow stream. At the next winding corner, I spot an American coot on the far side of a marsh, and closer to us, in the weeds, the red bill of a Moorhen. I look at John and raise my eyebrows. Little of this means anything to him, really, but when I point out the markings, show him the drawings in Sibley's, he's game and on the hunt. We cannot believe our luck as snowy egret, great egret, great blue heron, yellow-crowned night heron all appear on the edges of marsh, river, swamp, hidden slightly from view, but not impossible to spot. A wild turkey rushes across the path and we swerve down another detour across the gator culvert and end up lost in a field by a muddied stream dribbling into the Loxahatche. Looking up, the white Vs of swallow-tailed kites circle in the updraft while a red-shouldered hawk sits high on a deadened stump. We stop only for water, an almond bar, a little sustenance as we travel all the meandering paths, once, twice, sometimes in circles. Quietly whispering to each other, stopping, pointing, binoculars passed back and forth as I tell him what to look for. Whooping for glee along downhill paths, scattering scrub jays and grackles as we whiz by. We are children again, delighted with our mother's gift.

Grounded now, I carry my mother's *Sibley's*, her binoculars, and a thermos of coffee. There is no sighting without coffee — in kayaks or car or the edge of the river — a little "salut" to Mum who was never without coffee. While *Sibley's Guide to Birds* won't recompense my loss, it is a beginning, a link. I bring it with me, pack in it my knapsack as I leave the house for my morning river walk. Some pages have been welded together by water and gently pried apart, a palimpsest ghosted by time and travel. My walks are rambling, along familiar urban paths that follow the river and lead through ponds, inlets, underpasses. I put the earbuds away. Turn off the music. I am practicing being present.

Great Blue Heron

I take the highway west, aiming for a simple birding adventure, not too far from home, but far enough to distance me from family, responsibility, the pandemic. I have a small thermos of coffee, binoculars, bird book. The sacramental elements of remembrance on the fifth anniversary of my mother's death. I am headed out to bird, to consort with her spirit in the closest I can get to the northern flat rocky land of her childhood and comfort. The day is cool and gray. Quiet. For a moment, the pandemic has disappeared. There is only loss and a fecund promise of being. The parking lot is empty. I slip the knapsack on my back and veer off on a rocky trail full of tree roots and boulders and rising and falling ground. There is a flicker and a dark dart and the happy black and white of chickadees in the pine, the pin oak, the maple, the elm. All yellow and bright in the darkening sky. I hike up and down, around tree trunks and boulders, across boardwalks slightly sunken in the mud. A flit catches my eye, but no sighting, no matter how silent or long or still I stand on water's edge or deep in the forest. It is eerily quiet. Back at the car I am birdless and hungry. I grab the packed lunch and walk down a short path to a small rock outcrop on the shore. Small islets with single trees, bush dot the water. All is grey and brown and quiet. No riot of birds, no surprise sapsucker or grosbeak, just the mundane — the chickadee, an armada of geese, my own self. I break the bread, sink my teeth into cheddar. Crunch red apple. Then crack open the small thermos of black coffee that I have allowed myself today. I sit and breathe in my disappointment, the gray sky, the slightly rancid swamp smell. And let go of it all. Make myself praise: the redness of the apple, the pine needles on moss, the movement of muscles, the silence of my own being. I sit. This is, I think, what it is. A day of letting go. My eyes relax into the horizon, my breath into the cool air. Startled, a great blue heron rises in one sharp movement from the rock just meters from my seat. A strong languid beat of massive wings lifts her into the air. Her long beak sharp, undulating neck gracefully folding into body, broad wings slowly and powerfully pushing the air beneath her, long legs dangling. This great gray ghost ascends out of her reflection and glides past me toward the haze of the horizon.

I do not know when my mother will next appear, but I hold her lightly in my heart and know she soars. I am learning to look for wonders, miracles, thin spaces. Those liminal places where gaps crack open when a loved one dies. Then reappear. If we pay attention, slant. Catching a flick, a shift, on the periphery of our vision. If we hold a birder's eye to the world.

Mum's Dog

by James Burke

Dad never liked Mum's dog, but he only killed it by accident. He hit it with the car in our driveway, just as we got back home from football practice. He was telling me about the Dutch team in the '74 World Cup, when he shouted, "Jesus, fuck!" and the car bumped over something. He got out and bent down next to the front tyre on his side of the car. When I got out to look he said, "Jesus Billy, no, stay over there. You don't want to see this. Will you fetch a box from the garage?"

When I came back he'd lit a cigarette and was standing next to the car, looking up and down the street. "I don't think anyone saw," he said, taking the box. He knelt down again, and, looking over his shoulder, I could see the back legs of mum's white poodle, sticking out from under the tyre.

It hadn't been a very nice dog. It would pee on the carpet when it was scared, and it barked at everyone except Mum. She used to take it everywhere, but the noise drove everyone mad, so she'd leave it in the back garden when she went out. When me and Dad were at football, she'd go to visit Auntie Sally down the road, so the dog must have got out while we were all gone.

"Let the brake off and roll the car back a foot will you?" Dad said.

I'd driven the car before, sitting on his knees so he could do the pedals. Only around the industrial estate on a Sunday, but I knew how to do it. The driveway was sloped, so I didn't even have to start it. I just pulled the stick up with both hands until I could push the button in, then dropped it down as the car rolled backwards, and then pulled it back up with a crunch.

I got out, and Dad stood up with the box. He'd folded the cardboard flaps down, but one of the ears was poking out the side.

"Your ma doesn't need to know," he said, cigarette in his mouth. "She'd only be upset."

She'd be coming back to put dinner on soon though, so Dad put the box in the back of the car, and put the car in the garage, while I practiced keepy-ups in the drive.

"I didn't even see it," he said. "It just ran out. Bloody dog." He was just unlocking the front door when Mum came through the garden gate.

"God you're a mess," she said to me as she went inside. "You'll get straight in the bath!"

Dad stopped hiding the cigarette behind his back, stubbed it out on the bottom of his shoe and threw the butt towards the street.

"Come on, let's get cleaned up," he said. "We'll do something with the body later."

Mum worried about the dog all evening when she couldn't find it. She wanted us to go around the neighbourhood looking for it, but Dad said it was always getting out, it always came back, and she shouldn't worry. She went on her own though, but came back ten minutes later to see if the dog had come home while she was gone. She kept doing that, going out and coming back, but was never away long enough for Dad to take the car anywhere, so we just watched telly. At 10 o'clock mum told me to go to bed.

Dad stopped me as I was going up the stairs and said, "Sleep with your clothes on."

Mum was still calling for the dog in the back garden when I fell asleep.

I woke with a hand over my mouth and a light in my face.

"Quiet now," Dad said, and he took his hand away.

I pushed off the duvet, found my shoes and followed him down the stairs by torchlight. Dad opened the garage doors and we both got in the car. He took off the handbrake, the car rolled down the drive and onto the street. Then he started it and we drove back up the hill, past the house and turned left.

"Gave your ma a double brandy to steady her nerves," he said. "Always knocks her out."

He turned left again, and stopped the car by a house with a builder's skip outside. He got out, grabbed something from the skip and put it on the back seat. Twisting round in my seat I saw an empty, wooden box.

"Saw this crate the other day," he said, getting back in. "Thought we might find a use for it."

It was still warm, and we drove with the windows down. I'd never seen the streets so empty. We stopped next to the park. It was darker here, with tall trees blocking the streetlights. Dad took the wooden crate and left it next to the tall, iron railings of the park. Then he opened the boot of the car and handed me the torch to shine inside. He picked up the cardboard box with the dog in it, then hooked his finger around the handle of a petrol can and picked that up too. With his hands full he couldn't shut the boot, so he went to hand me the box.

"Ah, no," he said. "Maybe you'd better carry the petrol."

He gave me that, balanced the box on his leg and shut the boot. We went over to the railing and put everything down. Dad turned the crate on its side, so he could stand on it.

"Hang on to the torch," he said, and then picked me up under my armpits and swung me over the fence.

I dropped down the other side, and he passed me the petrol can, then the box with the dog in it. He pulled himself up onto the top of the railings, swung his leg over and dropped down the other side, getting his coat caught on the spikes at the top.

"Getting a bit too old for that," he said, reaching back through the railing to lift the crate up and over the fence after us. "This way," he said, taking the torch back and putting the petrol can in the crate. I picked up the cardboard box.

We followed a path until we got to a bandstand, then headed across the grass. There were no streetlights and everything was dark. When we heard a screech, Dad swung the torch round and lit up a fox, standing, looking straight at us. It watched us for a few seconds with glowing eyes, then walked away.

"Cocky aren't they?" Dad said. "That's why we can't just dump the body in a bin. They'd be at it straight away."

We walked downhill until we got to the big pond. There were trees on one side of it, and a stone edge all the way round.

"Maybe it wasn't such a bad dog," Dad said, putting the crate down and taking the petrol can out of it. "Your ma was fond of it anyway, so we'll give it a bit of a send-off".

He took the cardboard box from me, and handed me the torch to hold. He tore the flaps off the top of the box and pushed them into the crate. Then he tipped the dog out of the box into the crate, and ripped up the rest of the cardboard, which went on top of the dog.

"This is what the Vikings used to do when the chief died," he said, unscrewing the can and sloshing petrol into the crate.

The crate wobbled a bit as he lowered it into the pond, but it still floated. He stood up and took his cigarettes and lighter out of his coat. He lit one, took a long puff on it and blew out the smoke.

"May the road rise up to meet you," he said, and threw the cigarette into the crate.

Nothing happened. He lit another one and tried again, but the crate still didn't catch fire. It had floated away from the side a little, so he had to kneel on the stone wall and lean over to pull it back in. He splashed some more petrol into it, and then shook the can. It sounded almost empty, so he tipped the rest all over the sides of the crate. He pushed it back onto the water at arm's length, and then with one hand on the edge of the pond he reached out with his lighter. When he sparked it, the whole crate burst into flames, and dad pulled his arm back so quickly his other hand slipped, and he went into the pond up to his shoulder.

"Jesus!" he said laughing. "Now we're cooking."

The whole pond was lit up by the flames. He sat cross-legged on the grass and tested his lighter. It still worked, so he lit another cigarette, and I sat down next to him. The crate floated further away, the sparks from the fire drifting up into the sky.

"See, this way," he said, "we burn the evidence, and then it sinks." The fire fizzed and popped as we watched it.

The smoke was black, and smelt bad, but it was blowing away from us, and the breeze was pushing the crate across the pond, until it got stuck in some weeds. The flames were twisting around, taller than me, and reaching up into the branches of the tree above it. The thinnest branches glowed red, and then fell off into the water, but then the fire started to spread across the branches and into the rest of the tree. The leaves started to burn and drift into the air.

"Jesus," Dad said. He shone the torch into my face and then started laughing. "Have you ever seen anything like that?"

The tree was all flames now, and burning so fast it roared as it reached into the trees next to it. I could feel my cheeks getting warm.

"The dog's gone," Dad said, pointing the torch at where the crate had been.

The burning tree groaned, as the top of it split away and crashed to the ground, throwing sparks everywhere. It was like a bonfire.

"Oi!" we heard someone shout. "Who's there?"

Straight away, Dad switched off the torch, and held me still. I couldn't tell where the voice had come from.

"Run!" Dad said, and he scrambled onto his feet and took off, away from the pond.

I followed him, but once I was away from the fire I couldn't see a thing. I tripped, skidded onto my hands and knees and pulled myself up again. "Keep up!" I heard Dad shout ahead of me, but I kept stumbling and getting spun around. I thought I'd reach the bandstand, or hit one of the paths, but I never did. When I saw streetlights up ahead, I ran towards them, and found the fence. The street on the other side was much brighter than where we'd parked. I ran beside the railings, looking for Dad or the car.

I couldn't see a way out, until I found a bike chained to the other side of the railings. I pulled the frame tight to the iron bars and used it to climb to the top of the fence. With my hands and feet in between the spikes, I twisted myself around to climb down the other side. I got one foot onto the saddle, and was lowering myself down when the bike slipped over. I lost my grip, fell to the pavement and stumbled backwards into the road, just as the headlights of a car swerved towards me and stopped.

"Get in!" Dad shouted, and I did.

As we pulled away, I saw torchlight moving around the park, looking for us. Dad drove fast for a couple of streets, and then slowed down.

"You okay?" he said, reaching over and pulling my head around so he could see my face. "No bumps or bruises?" He was out of breath. "Jesus, I haven't had to run that fast in years," he said. "I should cut down on the fags."

He didn't say much else. We drove home a different way to when we left, so we were heading uphill to the house. Dad drove the car just fast enough so that when he turned into our driveway, he turned off the engine and lights, and the car still rolled all the way into the garage. I wondered if it had taken a lot of practice to be able to do it. He popped his door open, put a foot out of the car, and then looked back at me.

"Let's not worry your ma with any of this, eh?" he said, with his hand on my shoulder. Then he ruffled my hair, and got out.

Volcano

by Jeffrey Perkins

Roman is running the LA marathon.
It's no touch. No high fives. No kissing.
It's the time of the virus. What might

have been if the world responded
to gay death in the '80s with this level
of alarm? On the dance floor at Akbar

you are so beautiful. I watch other guys
look at you and hope you're going home
with me. And then you do and we sit

on my porch smoking pot and talking
about portals. You point out Venus
and I go back when we met, two years ago,

watching the stars drunk and high
on a stranger's lawn. Agnes Denes says
Anything important has to be almost

invisible. And underrated. And strong
enough to hold the earth. And I wonder

if you know, I'm thinking of you now.

You, in my bed, my hand on your inner
thigh, taking you in slow so later—now—
I can feel you when you're gone.

The runners and those watching are not
wrapped in protective suits. They are still
living their lives in the last open moments.

Every shape, every kind of movement.
I love them at this moment. I miss them
like I miss you. Mountain missing fire.

Held

by Sarah C. Baldwin

Lying next to me in the grass, Finn tilts his twitching nose upward, registering every smell — moles, I presume, and grackles and chipmunk and deer. As I read, he gazes at the field before us, a broad expanse of yellow grasses bordered by oaks and interrupted here and there by the gray hump of a granite boulder. Behind us, my husband and daughter are reading in the coolness of the little red house. We're spending the week away from Providence in this scruffy patch of western Rhode Island, on an old farm that belonged to my grandfather.

Finn, our eleven-year-old border collie, loves it here. In winter, I tell myself the ticks are dead and let him off his long tether. I love to watch him disappear into the snowy woods like an arrow. When he reappears at the back door he's exhausted and happy, with clumps of ice in the white fur of his paws.

But today it's hot. He's been moving sluggishly. On a whim I put my book down, stand, and unleash him. He gets up but doesn't run. He pants.

"You're acting like a tired old man," I say. "Come on, let's take a real walk."

I head down the dirt road and turn back. Finn walks slowly toward me, listing a little, then drifts to the side of the road where the poison ivy thrives. He squints into the bushes as though at a blackboard covered with equations he can't solve. The poisonous leaves brush his snout. He pants.

That night as my husband sleeps, I hear Finn click across the sunroom floor and whine at the screen door. I rise and let him out into a moonless night.

I follow, sweeping the damp grass with my toes in search of the tether. I attach him and return to bed. Before I fall asleep again, he's whining on the other side of the screen. I get up, detach him, let him in. We do this dance for hours. At some point deep in the night, I stop feeling sorry for him and start feeling sorry for myself. I lean down until my face is close to his and whisper-shout, "This has got to stop! I have to get up and go to work!" Impassive, Finn stares at my knees, panting. I feel mean.

The next day bursts open, clear and bright, the red of the barn like a trumpet blare against the blue, blue sky. For the moment, the press of July heat holds back, lying in wait. My husband and daughter are still asleep when I rise. I pull on a skirt and a sleeveless blouse but leave my feet bare. I'll step into shoes when I get to my office at the university. Finn stands in the sunroom, looking through the screen door. Did he ever lie down in the night, I wonder? I open the door and he steps out onto the grass and waits for me to attach him to the tether. I empty his water dish at the foot of the pear tree, fill it at the kitchen sink with cold water, and bring it back out. I crouch down, take his head in both my hands, and kiss the white stripe running up his snout.

"Be good, old man," I say, and his eyes lock on mine with the border collie laser-gaze. "Be well."

In the city, the streets are empty and the campus feels like it's napping. Most people have taken this Friday, wedged between July 4 and the weekend, as a vacation day, so the sunny halls of the modern building I work in are deserted. The air conditioned quiet is my reward for showing up, I tell myself. After a few hours of slow work, I call the house for an update.

My husband answers in what my mind registers, absurdly, as iambic pentameter: "Our Finn is not a happy dog." Earlier, my husband says, he took him to see Dr. Amy, the country vet up the road from the farm. When I ask what she said, my husband misses a beat. Then: "We'll talk about it when you get here."

My body feels concave, fragile. When I leave work, I walk carefully to the car so I don't crack.

***

My family hadn't planned to get a dog. But in the summer of 2001, when our children were ten and six, we were driving through the green fields and hills of Steuben County, New York, on our way home from my mother's house in Pittsburgh, and I noticed a sign beside the road that said SHEEPDOG TRIALS THIS WAY. Below the words was the unmistakable silhouette of a border collie's working crouch: rump in the air, front paw raised. We followed more signs down more country roads until we arrived at a flock of RVs cradled in a lush and shallow valley.

"Let's just take a look," I said as we got out of the car and headed toward a cluster of people.

A good distance away, a man in tall rubber boots blew a high-pitched whistle and a lithe, slinking border collie took off at a run. The dog zigzagged across the hillside, pushing a herd of sheep before it. Like a murmuration of starlings, the cloud of sheep spread and contracted, a solid form fluidly writhing, twisting on itself as the narrow-shouldered dog darted right, left, then right again, looping around the shape-shifting mass, climbing the hill and cutting back down to divide the flock in two, eventually driving each half into a different pen. All of it happened in silence under the expanse of cobalt sky. It was like watching TV with the sound turned off. I was mesmerized.

We wandered among the RVs, many of which had sheep or dogs in temporary pens beside them. The place smelled of hay and trampled grass and manure and fried dough. We stopped at a table with a banner that said *Glen Highland Farm Border Collie Rescue.* In a crate under the table a young, sweet-faced border collie was curled in sleep. My kids knelt to look at him. A woman wearing jeans and green rubber boots came over to us. She had Emmylou Harris hair and a no-nonsense air.

"Hi, I'm Lillie," she said. "Interested in adopting?"

I looked at my husband, who looked at me, smiling and resigned. I smiled back and turned to her.

"Thinking about it," I said.

Minutes later I was filling out forms, promising to fence our yard, describing the border collie I'd had as a child, hoping we would be approved as a rescue family.

"Is this reasonable? Are we ready for a dog?" my husband asked as we drove away, but he and I both knew it was too late to wonder.

"Yes yes yes yes yes!" the kids shouted together from the back seat.

A few weeks later, in early September, the phone rang. "I've got a couple dogs I want you to meet," Lillie said. "They've just arrived from a kill pound in West Virginia. When can you come?"

Toxic smoke was still rising from the ruins of the Twin Towers when we climbed in our minivan, left Providence, and headed west on the Massachusetts Turnpike. The children were quiet in the backseat. On the radio, E. L. Doctorow dolefully pondered the violence that had been done to his city, his voice full of sadness and restraint. But as the countryside enveloped us, the carnage grew more and more remote. *Welcome to the Berkshires* said a big blue sign. Another soon welcomed us to the Empire State. Gray barns and cone-topped silos floated past, and tired dirty-brick towns that had long ago abandoned their ambitions. In this newly wounded world, driving two hundred and fifty miles to rescue an abandoned dog felt like an absence of malice. It felt like the only thing to do.

Glen Highland consisted of barns, outbuildings, and a farmhouse at the bottom of a long dirt drive lined with bobbing heads of Queen Anne's lace. Fenced fields swelled in every direction. It looked like the definition for "farm" in a child's illustrated dictionary. Lillie emerged from the farmhouse and strode over to where we stood beside our car.

"Time to meet the dogs," she said. "Follow me."

She led us to one of the small barns and opened a door marked OFFICE. Inside were two shabby couches, an old metal desk, and the stinging pee smell of a place where animals are at home and people are mere guests. Lillie opened a door. A jittery young female with a glossy black coat shot into the room and sprang around it like a cricket, frenetic and indiscriminate in her enthusiasms. We all leaned forward to pet her but kept missing as she wriggled and bounced and whipped around in circles. After a while Lillie shooed her out and called for Finn. Another dog appeared in the doorway, hesitated, and then, staying low to the ground, slid into the room like a spy slinking between doorways. The dog eyed the couch where I sat, jumped up, and leaned his whole body against me. He did not make eye contact. He was like a boy asking a girl to dance while pretending he wasn't. I felt scared and in love. He continued to press against me.

"Looks like we'll take Finn," I said.

"That's right," Lillie said. "He just chose you."

***

I'd imagined Finn would fit instantly and seamlessly into our lives, but the first few days were rough. He came with a case of diarrhea, which meant hourly sorties throughout the first many nights. He could be fearful; he snapped at a man who bent to pet him on the sidewalk, and howled and thrashed during his first check-up at the vet.

One evening after dinner, as our kids went upstairs to do their homework and we braced for another diarrhea run, my husband said, "Do you think this was a good idea?"

I froze, hijacked by panic. My eyes widened.

"Of *course* it was a good idea," I sobbed. "Finn was *abandoned*, and now he has us, and we're his *family*, and we all *need* him, because loving him will make *us* all *better people!*"

I heard how overwrought I sounded but I couldn't stop crying. I was terrified — terrified because I secretly found this dog thing so much harder than I'd thought it would be. And terrified by the idea of giving Finn up.

***

Here is what I need to tell you: I, too, was adopted. Unlike Finn, though, I was not left in a box by the side of the road. In fact, the story I'd told myself my entire life — almost four decades — was that I'd been chosen. That my parents had waited and waited for me until at last there I was, a beautiful baby on a living room floor full of babies, and then they appeared, smiled and pointed at me as if I were a cupcake, and took me home, delighted.

Of course the story's not true, but that never kept me from believing it. That happy scene served as my protection. It became my identity. The refrain *I was chosen* drowned out the other words that must never be thought, much less spoken, even though they were buried somewhere in my body, everywhere in my body: *I had been given up.*

Suddenly, there in that kitchen — though I didn't understand it then — on some cellular level, my body remembered my abandonment.

This is not to say that at three months I was not brought home to loving parents and given a happy, stable, privileged life. But what about those first hundred days? What about that first day? That first night?

Like sleep, love has never been something I can bank. I am blessed to have been told *I love you no matter what, I will love you forever* (convincingly, ardently, earnestly, repeatedly), but I can't seem to store that love for another time, ready to be pulled out of my heart's back pocket on a bad day and applied where needed. I can't catch and absorb and *incorporate* it — make it part of my body, like food feeding muscle, like milk building bones. Though I am deeply, richly nourished by the many ways in which I'm lucky enough to be loved, some of that love will always leak through the fissure that cracked open when I was given away. Most of the time I don't think about this, because it's less a thought than a state of being, an inert fact lodged in my soma. But sometimes, when I feel unseen, or worse, unwanted, I instantly shrink back into that discarded baby in all her utter and infinite aloneness, a turtle on her back in the middle of the road under an eternal night sky.

But Finn: I knew I could love him boundlessly. I could love him with a ferocity that would mend his crack, soothe his hurt. I couldn't feel what it is to be unconditionally loved, but I could feel what it is to love unconditionally. I couldn't heal myself, but I felt I could heal him. And that was a consolation prize in the truest sense of the word.

The British psychoanalyst Donald Winnicott introduced the concept of the "holding environment," the literal and figurative gestures a mother makes that enable her baby to feel safe enough to come into being, to become herself. As I pleaded with my husband to be patient, promising to do everything I could to help the dog adapt, I felt the intense and desperate need for Finn to know — really *know* — that he was seen and loved and safe forever. Countless times over the next ten years, I would sit beside him, throw one arm across his shoulders, and trace and retrace that white stripe on his head, whispering a world of love in his ear. In the beginning, I think, I was his holding environment. But as time went on, he became mine, too.

***

I speed down I-95 toward the farm, the dread that Finn won't be there sitting heavily on my chest. The year before, he had suddenly become very sick, and I'd had to face the idea that he might actually die. Now the possibility of his death is no longer new, and I find it slightly easier to grapple with an enemy that is not unfamiliar. So much so that as Providence disappears in my rearview mirror, a thought catches me by surprise: *If Finn has died, I will bury him.* Though my insides have always crazed like hot glass under water at the mere sight of him in distress, *I will bury him* makes me feel intact, even brave.

I brace myself for the turn onto the dirt road, the red house and red barn and the stretch of grass between them without Finn on it.

But he is there.

He is sitting up, panting with his mouth open wide, like he's smiling and sticking his tongue out at me at the same time. He does not come to greet me with his whole body wagging. But he is there.

My husband comes outside. My daughter does not, which confirms what I already know: the news is bad.

"Finn is full of cancer," my husband says when I get out of the car. "Dr. Amy says you can come talk to her in the morning."

I look at our feet in the grass. I can feel my husband watching me. He's right to expect tears. But strangely I don't cry. I just hug him, nodding into his shoulder. We stand like that for a long time.

That evening dinner is a subdued affair. Sweet Rhode Island corn on the cob seems a frivolous food to be eating, but we do, chewing diffidently. I think we feel guilty for knowing what Finn doesn't. We are patient with his restless comings and goings. We abide the constant panting. While my husband clears the table, I slip Finn a steak bone and go sit with him in the grass while he gnaws it.

"You're so handsome, Finny. All the ladies say so." I stroke his ears with my hands.

The next morning I drive the quarter mile to Dr. Amy's home, where she tells me what she told my family the day before.

"Finn's mostly healthy, but the x-rays show a tumor that's filling his chest. He's panting because every bit of his being is focused on getting more oxygen. The tumor's squeezing his lungs into tangerines," she says, making two fists to show me. She can't fix it, she says. She can try to make him comfortable for as long as we want her to, but it's a losing proposition.

I'm grateful for her frankness. There is no wait-and-see. Suffocation is the fast-approaching finish line. I have a fleeting image of my proud, square-chested fellow rescue tipping over sideways as he gasps for air.

"I understand."

"Would you like me to come to the house at the end of the day?" she asks.

It takes me a second to grasp what she's offering to do.

"Yes, please."

In that moment, I know everything the day will hold. I will dig a grave. We will love Finn lavish amounts. He will die in the late afternoon.

I stop by the pond that is tucked in the land between Amy's house and ours. I make a wish that the great blue heron will be there. Sure enough, he's standing on the shore, long necked and putty colored with touches of slate blue. He sees me and ascends without ado, a majestic thing, his wings flapping languorously, his neck folding itself into an S, his long legs straight out behind him. He rises in slow, widening circles, and then, as though released from the spiral, he flies due west, up, up, up over the aspens and pines, and disappears. I stand there a while, forcing myself to hold the notion of Finn's death in my mind to see if I can bear it.

***

The location of the grave is easy to choose. Only fifty feet from the house, it is visible from the places where we spend most of our time — the sunroom and kitchen and pear tree. It is the place where Finn used to disappear into the woods when I let him run in the winter and the place where he'd emerge again, exhilarated and wide eyed and wolfen. Spongy with star moss, the spot lies under a slender but tall white chestnut whose long-fingered leaves will form a sheltering canopy.

Even though I have never dug a grave before, I figure it out fast. I slice my spade into the earth, lift the dirt, and place it to the side. I do this again and again and again for long minutes, until I've marked out a rectangle slightly longer and wider than the body that will go in it. Then I simply dig out that shape with a shovel. I slice through tough, stringy roots and pull out pieces of old terra cotta pipe and fist-size rocks. I try to make the walls more or less straight and the bottom flat. I'm lucky; I have all day to dig this grave, and the day is taking its time. Finn ambles over. His panting is relentless, but eventually he finds a way to lie down nearby, propped up Sphynx-like, his head erect. I know he doesn't know he is watching his own grave being dug, but a hushed contrition inhabits me just the same. And yet, the slow digging is weirdly consoling. It feels reverent. It is as small, quiet, and unassuming as an act can be and still be holy.

I dig and dig, and while I do I talk to Finn about the day, point out the flitting dragonflies, comment on how beautiful and clear the air is and how distinguished he looks. I dig and dig and dig until I look up and realize that I am standing in a grave.

Still panting, Finn rises and moves to sit in the shade of the Norwegian pine. He's backlit by the sunlight gilding the western field, where the thrushes dip into the knee-high grass. His long quivering tongue has taken on a brickish cast, but his saliva is clear and drips from his tongue like water. The more desperately he pants, the wider his smile becomes. His eyes are bright, slightly wild looking, even blind. He snaps at the occasional deer fly. The air cools.

In all the world there is no finer smell than the smell of Finn's paws. They are white, and each is adorned with a little tuft of fur. The pads are scratchy-rough and the fur between them improbably soft, and the smell is the happiest thing I've ever smelled. They are sometimes cool and damp and sometimes warm, but they always smell deliciously of clean dirt, like something fundamental and good and safe and right. I lie next to him now where he sits in the grass and caress the tufts with my fingers. I gently lift a paw to my nose. It smells of my other favorite smell, the pond — wet, slightly metallic, elemental — where Finn had waded just the day before.

In the early days, just after he came to live with us in the city, Finn would sometimes escape into the wooded park across from our house. Once, he disappeared for hours. We kept vigil on our front steps.

At one point my husband murmured, "What are we going to do if he doesn't come back?"

My little girl raised her hands and let them drop. "Die," she sighed.

Now a teenager, she comes out of the house and walks over. She drops to her knees and buries her nose in another paw. Finn obliges. We are comforted.

The phone rings.

"Vet's on her way," my husband says.

I hold Finn's paw tighter. A hummingbird dives into the mass of orange flowers on the trumpet vine growing by the barn. A few minutes later we hear a car door opening. I lift my head to see Amy walking toward us holding a black satchel, like a doctor on TV.

"Hi everyone. Hey, Finn." Her smile is warm and a little melancholic. She looks at each of us. "I thought we could talk for a little bit. But first I'm going to give Finn a tranquilizer to help him relax."

My husband gently holds Finn's head while Amy gives him a shot in his rump. We arrange ourselves in a semi-circle in the grass. We don't look at each other. We stare at Amy as though our survival hangs on her words. She speaks softly and clearly, like a teacher or a funeral director, passing her hand back and forth over the tips of the grass as if it were braille.

"I'm going to shave a small patch of fur from Finn's foreleg so I can insert a shunt. That's where I'll inject something called pentobarbital. In less than a minute the drug will send him into what I call a plane of deep unconsciousness. It's like a state of profound relaxation. It will be so deep that all his major organs will stop working." She looks up at us and then continues. "Because of the tumor, there's a small chance that at that moment, fluid will come out of his mouth. It could be clear or green, and it could be mixed with blood. You might notice a reflexive breath or a muscle twitch."

She adds that his eyes won't close.

We nod, each of us a child.

She reaches into the bag and withdraws an electric shaver, the kind barbers use for crewcuts, or to neaten up the neck. Finn has been weaving among us, resisting the tranquilizer's effects. Suddenly his legs fold under him and he's down. He stares at the trees across the road, still panting. I kneel beside him, caressing the length of his body. *OK, Finn, it's OK*, my hands say. Amy clicks on the electric shaver and in one small upward movement bares a little area of skin on his leg. I make myself watch the beveled edge of the shunt enter his vein. Finn doesn't flinch. Amy inserts the needle into the shunt. It's fat, like a truncated turkey baster, and filled with blue fluid. She holds it in one hand and presses the plunger slowly with her other palm. She presses hard, as though against resistance. My hands are spread wide and flat on Finn's side. *If only my hands were bigger,* I think, *I could hold you completely.* Then, under my palms — the merest breath, a slight heave of the ribs, an exhale. The dog's body goes still. I look at his mouth, watching for a stream of fluid. None comes. His beautiful brown eyes remain open. This cheers me briefly; it's as though he is still there. With both hands I caress him from snout to ruff, over and over. I whisper his name. My tears land on his head, like Rapunzel's on the prince's face after he's fallen into the briars. I am hoping he knows what I'm dying for him to know, hoping, absurdly, that he is aware of us there with him. I remain intent on caressing him, on feeling him under my hands. Willing him to feel me. *I'm not ready, after all,* I think, *I need five more minutes. I need to tell him one thousand more times how utterly he is loved, I need to make sure he knows he's not being abandoned.* Somewhere in me is the seed of a feeling that even in this endless, slow-rising day, I have fallen short. The feeling grows into a thought, but it is too late for doubt or remorse or declarations or even one last look in the eye, and the thought dies.

Amy leans forward and places the stethoscope on the white triangle of Finn's chest. She stares past him into the grass, listening. The tilt of her head looks sorrowful, as though from inside him Finn's heart is telling her something terribly sad in the smallest voice in the world. After some minutes, she takes the stethoscope out of her ears.

"Would you each like a bit of fur?" We nod. She deftly clips some from Finn's ruff, a tuft for each of us, and one for our son, who lives far away.

"Could you please also clip this?" I ask, stroking the spray of fur on his left back foot. She does.

"We call these toe slippers," she says, smiling as she places the curl of white fur in my palm.

Still crying, I stand and get the faded beach towel I've put just inside the door. Amy and I bend to shift Finn's substantial, still-supple body onto it. When we lift it, her side is higher than mine and the dog's head flips back disturbingly, folding flat against his body like an origami crane. I have the rear, so I raise my end of the towel a little more, and his head flops back to its natural position.

Amy and I make our way down the grassy slope to the grave, Finn slung between us. My daughter is crying and her father is trying not to. I step down into the hole and with Amy's help lower Finn carefully to the dirt floor. Down here, the thought of covering him with earth suddenly seems barbaric. But I'm afraid if I stop I won't be able to continue. I need to protect his beautiful face, with its white stripe and knowing eyes, the face that is his alone, the face we've looked at and loved for so many years, the face that was smiling at me less than an hour ago. Awkwardly straddling his body, I fold a corner of the towel over his head. Then I reach up and take a shard of terra cotta pipe, using it to slide some earth down onto him from the pile beside the grave. I reach up and my husband grasps my hand and helps me climb out. We all take turns lowering shovelfuls of dirt onto his body with exquisite tenderness. But no matter how gently we do this it feels violent and final. Finn is about to be literally, irrevocably gone. Watching him disappear under the dirt is far worse than holding him as he died. I want to beg his pardon, not for stopping his heart but for putting him underground. I can't find words.

Oh, Finny.

Oh, Finn.

Back in our house in the city, I stare through the skylight at the new moon and weep for our dog, alone and helpless under the silencing weight of the cold earth. His absence is as tangible as a presence. Again and again I step into the backyard where he spent his days and slam into a void like a force field. My husband says he hears Finn's nails clicking on the hardwood floors in the night.

And yet, weeks later, something shifts. It's another warm, fully realized summer day. Sitting on the back steps after work, I suddenly realize I'm not picturing Finn dead, Finn buried, Finn entombed. I'm not talking to him in my head, promising we haven't forgotten him. Instead, in my gut a strange and quiet gladness begins to bloom, as though something wonderful has happened and I'm the only one who knows it. I am cradling Finn's memory. *Is it his good life I'm holding, or his gentle death? It is both of those things*, I think, and it is also him alive inside me, our union no longer marred by suffering. All that's left is the essence of what mattered, the uncomplicated knot of our connection.

In the afterlife from a distant forest

by Vivian Eyre

driftwood cast upon the sea's lashing,
slips through the fingers of waves,
colonized by gribbles, riddled with
pinholes from shipworms, hoppers,
wood piddocks home/dinners, dressed
in brine at the wrackline — a woman
tosses driftwood into a pile of dunnage,
salvage bound for the old port dock.
On the dock, a man finds driftwood,
sunbaked, salt-smooth, the size of
a long-bone. Like Odin, he commands
the wood to: *Cavort. Frolic. Frisk About.*
The man's lover strokes the wood's scars,
whorls, burled knots, deep striations in
chalk, wood ash, tinge of smoke,
singed quill feather gray. At her shop,
she twists lady orchids around the wood,
rhythms yellow petals into a dancing vine.
Drift, drift, drifting out of itself — I stare
in the shop window, my reflection shifts.
It's low tide. Waves fall & bloom what floats.
That sparkler. Earth's flint catching my breath.

Holobiont

by Ann Stout

Holobiont. Agustín Fuentes gave me this new word at the beginning of the New Year, during the *On Being* podcast with Krista Tippet titled "This Species Moment." Here is what he said:

> The holobiont . . . this is this basic concept, that organisms are, ourselves, things, cells that are made up of our own DNA and proteins and all of that — plus thousands, tens of thousands, maybe hundreds of thousands, of other organisms and their DNA, simultaneously. So we are ourselves ecosystems . . . the idea that these holobionts move around in the world, interacting, shedding, sharing, overlapping, fusing — it sounds like a science fiction movie.

What a concept! A new way of seeing, of being, of defining my space and place in this world. A new way to think of myself, not defined by inches or pounds, or by my blood type or my DNA. Not defined by my external age which so poorly reflects my inner age. I am still so young on my journey towards selfhood, or otherhood, or wholeness, or Holiness.

As a Holobiont I am a composite of microorganisms, of memories, of enculturation, of habit. I am connected to the Holobiont of others — sharing their air, their organisms, their thoughts, their feelings, and their lives. Most of the time I coexist peaceably. But sometimes conflict erupts — my gut rebels against me, or I rebel against others.

I am still filling in holes in my being. As a writer I work to string things together, to fill in the gaps of my understanding. Every time I question the meaning behind something I can come up with many different answers and sometimes make space for them all to coexist.

Holo… whole, holey, holy… Sometimes the holes, the missing parts, add up to the whole and there is a sacred mystery about it — the silence between the notes, the darkness separating stars. To take that all in and discover that it is more than just the sum of its parts is a step towards a Holo-understanding, a Holo-cognition.

Apoptosis was another word that opened worlds — a scientific word describing the process of programmed cell death that exists in all living things. This word offered an explanation of why we cannot live forever, why our Holobionts ultimately fail. Most of the cells in my Holobiont die and are replaced — from the fast gut and skin cells to the slow bone and brain cells. I am interested in the process of continual cellular rebirth, the daily reincarnation of most of our being. Every morning our brain rises from the death of sleep to alertness. The Buddhist concept of reincarnation into other beings is not so far-fetched in this framework. We are born again, and again, and again. Starting over and over and over.

Westerners often prefer things to be concrete and not abstract. The mystery of death is frightening. We cannot control what we do not understand. We like to be in charge of the whole.

My physician husband John once came home and shared an interesting patient encounter. "Interesting patient encounters" are often defined by: making a difficult diagnosis that makes you look good; seeing something you have never seen before; having an emotional exchange that breaks through your clinical straitjacket; or feeling angry at something beyond your control. Sometimes it is something that makes you question your assumptions.

A family had brought in their child with Batten's Disease, an inherited retinal and neurological deterioration leading to blindness and early death. This child's Holobiont was doomed by a small genetic code change. A spark dropped on a dry forest floor. It is a horrible diagnosis, but genetic counseling and testing can sometimes avoid having an affected child. John sat down with the family to break the bad news and explain the diagnosis and its ramifications. The family listened calmly.

"Oh, we know that," the father reassured John when he finished. He explained that they knew their family carried this gene and that marrying his cousin had increased the chance of having an affected child. It was an outcome they were willing to accept in service of preserving the family wholeness — the Holobiont of their clan and community. Their culture put clan over individuality, community wholeness over a single person. This is almost always viewed in our westernized medical world as a poor choice. An uneducated choice. An avoidable choice. And yet, it makes me think.

I think about the beautiful family I saw on a medical mission trip. Another boy with an inherited neurological disorder. This boy had made the news in Bolivia at the time of his diagnosis because of the rarity of the condition. Being newsworthy in medicine implies either very good or very bad news. His was bad. They came wanting more information about how they could help their beloved child. It was probably the same reason the other family had come to see John. They knew there was no cure, but tugged at any nibbles on the lines of hope cast out from their doomed liferaft.

We sat in the small room set aside to examine the kids. The well-dressed young parents handed me the thick medical chart they had brought with them. I flipped through, looking for English signposts to explain what was causing this boy's obvious delay, the awkward wide-based gait, the tremor of his hands as he reached for a toy, the saliva that slipped out of the corner of his five-year-old mouth when he slowly smiled. I finally found it — Pelizaeus Merzbacher Disease. A beautiful phrase with which to nail a coffin closed. A fatal mitochondrial disease passed on through the Holobiont of the mother to the boy, first incorporated into her DNA as a bacteria so far back in the genetic code that the word generations may not apply.

I set aside the chart and put my hand on the mother's hands clenched tightly together in her lap.

"I'm sorry," I said as tears welled in my eyes. "I don't think there is anything else we can offer now."

The parents leaned into each other in shared grief as they felt the taut line of hope going slack again. As I gave them time to absorb this new disappointment I watched the older sister entertain the boy. She picked up a pink rubber pig from the cardboard box holding my equipment and showed it to him, speaking with a soft high voice as though to an infant. He watched her and smiled, wobbled a bit in his chair, and reached to pick up a yellow chicken toy from the box. The dark waters of their journey suddenly glowed with bioluminescence. Life manifesting itself through love. Flashes of wonder if you take the time to look for them. This family Holobiont was well and thriving. The weakness of one member, the betrayal of one mitochondrion would not be their downfall. This girl would grow up with a level of compassion that would ripple through the Holobiont of her community, and balance the sacrifice of this boy. With a full heart, I turned to offer another hope, another tug on the line.

"New gene therapies are always being explored, and something may come up to help your son."

Then I added the most important part. "Alejandro is lucky to be in such a caring family who can give him the best life possible. He is blessed to have this beautiful sister and both of you as parents."

The mother knew the painful truth that the defect had come through her. Earlier she had worriedly asked me about trying to figure out why she had the problem in her genes.

"It doesn't matter how it happened." I tried to reassure her. I realized my medical authority gave me zero ability to advise her on her personal journey of suffering, but I would give what I could. "What is important is that you love him and take care of him as much as you clearly do."

She smiled weakly through her tears.

I sent them away with a small consolation prize — a prescription for new glasses which they could easily afford to buy in an optical shop. Later in the day, I was surprised to see them waiting their turn just like everyone else to get a second-hand pair from the donated supplies. The people in line with them were enjoying watching the children play. The parents saw me, smiled, and thanked me again. I was reminded that the value of a gift does not lie in its cost or scarcity, but in the intent of the giver, and the hidden hole in the recipient that the gift may fill.

Holobiont. It's a good word. I like it better than apoptosis.

An Absence in the Air

by Kelly Hevel

I'm watching from my flat as the men fell the tree. Since I moved to this
Istanbul neighborhood five years ago, it has swayed outside my sixth-floor
windows, rooted in the garden below that stretches the length of the city
block. Surrounded completely by the backs of apartment buildings, the
garden is patrolled by a troop of noisy cats, but it's rare to see people there.

Today, upon arriving home, at first I didn't notice the absence in the air
outside as I slid out of my shoes and tore off my bra in the usual post-work
ritual. Moving from room to room, I slowly became aware of a persistent
shouted conversation outside my windows and the sound of neighbors
calling to each other from windows and balconies.

***

An American transplant in Turkey, I have learned to live in community
in a new way. In our Istanbul homes we pretend we don't know what's
going on inside the homes of others. It is considered poor form, a kind of
showing off, to not have curtains on your windows. This is something we
foreigners sometimes choose to ignore when we live in an apartment like
mine, which is high enough that there are no sight lines to allow a stray
glance inside. But some are scandalized by this behavior, and you may even
get a talking to by a neighbor trying to help you out with the advice to add
some sheer curtains for the sake of propriety.

The invisibility of home life is a respite from the unrelenting interactions
that form the public life of Turkey. Once outside the confines of your
home, you are part of the hive-like life of the city, like it or not. Strangers

will talk to you, laugh with you, give you advice, pat your children on the head. It is normal to ask a stranger for help parking, or for an old woman on an icy street to be passed from stranger's arm to stranger's arm as she makes her way home, each of us taking our turn helping her on her way before we turn off her path and onto our own, handing her with a parting smile, but no comment, to the next helper. I've seen many people help a blind person with an obstacle but never once have I seen them ask permission. It is a given that help will be given and accepted, often without comment or fuss from either party.

As I follow the discourse on the rights and preferences of people with disabilities in the United States I wonder what an American would think of a stranger wordlessly taking their arm to steer them around a low-hanging branch they can't see, then walking silently on. In Turkey, there is a different awareness of and perspective on the needs and comfort of all the parts of the whole. Once, riding a crowded bus, I was standing in the aisle holding a strap when an older "auntie" became agitated because I didn't have a seat. I told her I was fine, but she wasn't having it and proceeded to rearrange people, pointing and directing, until eventually she somehow managed to create an empty seat beside herself for me. Not one person questioned her directions, they all complied without comment, until I was eventually seated beside her as she offered me a fig from the small paper bag she was holding. There was really no choice but to eat the fig. Accepting hospitality is as important as offering it here.

***

I am used to sounds echoing off the walls of the buildings surrounding the central gardens below my flat, gardens which are inaccessible to all but a few of the ground floor inhabitants who mostly choose to ignore them. We all know we can hear each other through our open windows, we hear the tinkle of spoons on tea glasses in the morning and the complaints of children arguing with their parents in the afternoon, but we pretend we can't to preserve our city privacy. Now and then I accidentally lock eyes with a woman on the balcony perpendicular to mine hanging her laundry as I water my geraniums, and we both look away quickly to maintain the illusion of solitude. We are used to each other's voices and habits and no longer notice them consciously. But today the awareness that unfamiliar voices have been shouting continuously outside has filtered through, and I have come to the window to investigate.

Though my apartment is six floors up there has always been a very tall tree embracing the entire flat, stretching its arms from the bedroom window and balcony across to the windows in the living room. I've often been startled by the flexible treetop blowing wildly from side to side, high above its firmly planted base. In the winter moonlight its bare branches run from one side of the wide windows to the other with the wild winds blowing in from the Bosphorus. Out of the corners of my eyes I have seen flashes of motion, and in irrational moments of fear, before common sense takes hold, I have been frozen in place, thinking someone has run past, close to my windows. Then I remember how high up I am and giggle as my heart rate slows. The stately tree has provided a green cover over the years, the leaves a welcome shelter from prying eyes and a rare reminder of timeless nature just an arm's length away.

Now, walking down the hallway toward the sound of men's voices, I see an unfamiliar emptiness in the air outside, spreading from one end of the apartment to the other. Even before I reach the windows I feel exposed to the blank, pale sky.

I rest my arms on the windowsill and lean out, echoing the stance of neighbors in the surrounding buildings. Looking down, we watch the men with their web of ropes running from backyard to backyard, across walls and through trees, holding the old giant in place as they finish the job of bringing it down. The gardens of several buildings are littered with the remnants of the graceful arms of the tree. One man is standing below the denuded stump, the raw end of which still stretches to the height of two men. He alternates between shouting to those surrounding the tree and turning his chainsaw on it, causing small pieces to fly into the suffocating air.

We watch as ropes are secured to guide the fall of the remaining body of the tree. From my perspective, it seems the tree is still too tall and will take down a garden wall when it goes. I wonder if the men are too close to see clearly what they are doing. Eventually I grow bored watching the arm waving and shouting, and I retreat inside, but soon after I hear a crash and return to my post at the window to see that the tree trunk has indeed fallen on a garden wall, shattering it. Later, I look down and see all evidence of the tree is gone, but the pieces of the wall remain, scattered in the gardens.

This tree I shared with my neighbors sheltered us from summer sun and neighborly eyes as we sat on balconies mere feet apart, barely clothed, hoping for a breeze. It provided us not just with shade, but with a fragile scrim of privacy that grew thicker in the summer when we emerged to take the air and thinned out with the falling leaves in the autumn when we began to retreat to the warmth of our homes. We watched together as it was taken down. Now, we are exposed and will have to be careful where we direct our gaze when we go out into our shared living space if we want to maintain the polite pretense of neighborly privacy.

**

When you become a native of a big city — because let's face it, that's what it is, it's often a becoming; in most cities it's rare to be born a native — it's the disappearance of small things that sticks you in the ribs, because it's the small things that make you feel you belong. Visitors don't notice the little shops on the corner but those shops on the corner, and the men and women who run them, are an important part of our local community. When one disappears it leaves a hole bigger than the empty storefront. It was when the corner shop closed in my old neighborhood that it became unlivable. I missed the patience of the guys there when I forgot the Turkish word for honey and instead buzzed like a bee, but more than that, without the guys running the shop and their cohort of friends on the street at night I no longer felt safe. One night a man grabbed me while I was unlocking my door and I ran after him shouting angrily. When I realized there was no one to hear, no more neighbors sharing my street, just a stream of tourists coming and going in short-term rentals, I knew it was time to move on.

Change is inevitable, and sometimes necessary. While our tree was green and lush outside my windows, I used to look at the huge, dead branches two floors down and hope the winds never twisted enough to send those branches through someone else's windows. I'm sure we are all safer now that the tree is gone, but the removal of something as small as only one tree shifts, ever so slightly, the relationships of dozens. Ironically, the removal of its sheltering curtain serves to isolate us as we adjust to unfamiliar exposure. I notice my neighbor darting inside when I appear outside, and I back away quickly when I see her come out to hang clothes. Without the tree between us it seems as if we are in closer proximity, and we have to renegotiate our relationship to each other and our environment. We feel exposed when we are caught on our balconies, they no longer feel like extensions of our private home space now that the green wall between us is gone. These small changes change our relationships, how we move through the city and where we feel protected from the eyes and actions of others.

Like ancient city walls, trees rise and fall, leaving empty spaces behind to be filled with some unknown future. The tree was here before us, but now we remain, responsible for adapting to the empty space it left until we too disappear and are replaced. What will we fill our shared space with? Will it separate us or bring us closer together?

***

I've learned to be comfortable with the roles and responsibilities of public life in the collectivistic Turkish culture. Living in cities on the east coast of the U.S. I've always felt that, while we know our neighbors are close, we tend to ignore that physical closeness. We cultivate a pretense of ignorance in order to respect each other's privacy, and this urge to remain psychically separate even when physically close extends outside our homes. American culture is more centered on individualism and self-sufficiency, so sitting on the subway or walking down a crowded city street we cling to our privacy, avoiding eye contact and interactions.

The absence outside my window has made me realize that the comfort I've come to feel with the collective public life of Turkish society only increases my sense of discomfort when our private lives collide. It took some time, but now that I have adjusted to the closeness of the public sphere in Turkey, its contrast with the privacy of home life feels odd. Now that I've been conditioned to reach out when I see a stranger on the street, it seems strange when a neighbor on a balcony turns away.

***

A timeless peace radiated from that tree gently blowing side to side. In the first treeless summer, the sun beat relentlessly on my apartment, a daily reminder of the loss of its protective veil. Two months after the tree fell, I looked into the garden below and found the stump was invisible, hidden by the new young leaves and branches that had sprung from it.

Plans

by Amy Glynn

I don't like to plan, but I want to have a plan. I want that feeling of security before heading into a situation, a to-do list in my pocket, reminders scratched on post-it notes, a google calendar mapping out my day. Inevitably, the plan will fall apart, along with the false sense of security that what comes next can be controlled. But that doesn't stop me from wanting one.

The plan was to move to DC for a summer internship to be closer to my then girlfriend. We were still in the too-soon-to-live-with-each-other-yet-see-each-other-every-night stage, so I jumped on Craigslist to search for housing leads. I researched furnished apartments within walking distance of downtown. Calls were made, landlords were contacted until I found a place that was overpriced with a four-month minimum commitment.

At the last minute, I got word that my girlfriend's friend of a friend was subletting their place. It was a bit farther away but in a quirkier neighborhood called Mt. Pleasant with gay roommates. No commitments, no forms to sign, so instead of asking more questions, I said let me know when I can move in. That's how I ended up living in a nudist, gay commune over a sticky DC summer.

The place was owned by two older men who called each other Mister and slept in their second-floor bedroom with the door wide open. They kept compost in yogurt containers in the kitchen, which attracted black flies and exuded a strong smell. I once opened the oven in search of some pans (the logical place to store things) when I discovered a hard, green substance inside. The oven hadn't been turned on since I'd arrived two months before. Pizza? I thought as I grabbed some old newspaper to throw it away.

I lived with the Misters, two other men, and a woman who was my roommate for about a week before the woman moved out into a nicer (read: clothing required) apartment downtown. As plans go, my girlfriend ended up moving back home due to a health scare just as I was moving into this unfamiliar place with no AC. But it was too late to find another internship so I stayed. My roommates and I made a habit of lying on the basement floor after dinner to stay cool. We would spread out with as much bare skin as possible touching the cool ceramic tiles, breathing in the dusty air.

We shared one bathroom among the five of us. It was one of those European-style wet baths where everything in the bathroom can (and did) get wet. The shower head was directly over the toilet and a plant hung from the ceiling that would brush against my shoulders. I had to remember to close the toilet lid and leave the TP outside each time I showered. Otherwise, if I forgot, I was left standing in a puddle of pee water with soaked TP. There was a small sink on one side and a drain in the middle of the floor. The bathroom was on the second floor and whenever the shower was turned on a pipe leaked by the kitchen. It sounded like summer rain.

I had a tiny room in the attic on the third floor. It was so hot up there I felt like I was sleeping next to the sun. I had three fans that blew in my face, kicking up debris that stuck to my white shirt like a swarm of gnats.

In the mornings, the Misters would make me a coffee with latte art in the shape of intricate geometric designs. I wouldn't dare drink it until I'd put it in the fridge to cool. I'm not sure my body could ingest any more heat without boiling over. I got in the habit of sucking on frozen peas throughout the day, leaving a trail of water drops wherever I went.

When the other female roommate moved out, I was jealous at first. She had gone back to a planned, meticulous life with clean counters, cool air, and clothes. When she invited me to her new place for a housewarming party, I jumped at the chance. I put on a stringy dress and arrived with my seven layered vegan dip and a bag of chips in tow. We sat on oversized couches with beautiful displays of cheese and olives spread out on an expensive looking board. Someone opened the bag of chips I brought and dumped them into a wooden bowl. They served wine in actual glasses, handed out cloth napkins, and ate with metal silverware. They spoke in the DC chatter I despised, asking what I did for work, which school I went to, how many letters were after my name. After about an hour, I realized I was the only one eating my dip. I admit it may have been hard to distinguish the seven distinct layers that melted on my walk over (they were all there: guacamole, refried beans, salsa, cashew cheez, nutritional yeast, lettuce, and peppers), but it was food all the same. As I packed up my things to head out, someone handed me my plastic tub of dip. I got goosebumps on my arm when our hands touched. The place was too cold for me anyway.

I returned to the feverish apartment of exposed skin. My roommates were lying on the couch so I joined them and offered them some dip. They ate it by the spoonful and told me about their day. They were unkempt and hairy, with red bumps and soft spots.

I became familiar with A's birthmark on his behind, how R's skin was like chicory root, slippery and rough. The way C seemed to have a line of hair from the tip of his head down to between his butt cheeks as if someone had drawn it with a pencil. Their bare asses left sweat marks on the kitchen chairs in the shape of elephant ears. They walked around as if they had never known what it was like to be covered and taught me what a self could be like, unclothed.

Surfeit

by DeMisty D. Bellinger

This is where we are now:
I dreamt of mold spreading
throughout our house. It grew,
soft and bunny fuzzy white
beneath dishes, in the sink,
on the back of our hands.

In real, waking life,
mold grows atop the moss
outside because it won't stop
raining. And when the sun
shines, it's humid and hot.
And when it doesn't rain—

I imagine fungus, mold
overtaking a mistreated earth
growing between our toes
or in patches of ringworm
on our faces. We know the biggest
organism is a kind of mushroom,

expanding underground.
This armillaria,
this honey fungus, covers
acres and is older than
the oldest tree or tortoise.

This is where we are now:
sweating in a deluge
of hurricane rains,
practicing the Sisyphean
task of ridding ourselves
of tenacious growth.

Autumn's Bones

by Sage Ravenwood

Tumble wind green leaf dance   tiny shadows
crawling asphalt and worried faces
Echoes of too soon spiraling   across
     a Walgreen's parking lot   Too bright
     last of summer sun glinting off a line of windshields
Needle prick a bark less Armageddon
Tempest tapping on the windowpane
Come you Autumn   whistle through the tree bones
of limbs raked of umber foliage   in this season
of dead things falling   Rattle your oracle bones
shake those pieces of ox scapula and turtle plastron
          of our human affliction   Listen to the creak and sway
As a Zephyr blows through branches armature grasp
for dark skies graying hope   Down   down we go   Below
the antler rut deer markings   Our sunless flayed bark
          buried dirt deep beneath the winds moan
          to roots tangled in skulls of afterthought
Whispers rattling terra firma's ribcage
knees thunder cracked   floor mopped tears
Our hand wringing finger splayed remorse
          skeletons bemoaning the winds rancid truth
Lungs long bleached of breath singing
come brittle soothsayer   Listen closely
as the wind speaks and the land talks back

Jaguar

by Beto Caradepiedra

Bocas Del Toro, Panama 1931

In the house where Mama got sick, we five children, all under the age
of twelve, waited for our fathers. Mama was a troupe singer and dancer.
Dancer headwrap and dancer feet. Dancer fingers and dancer gaze. Now
she faced death at the age of thirty-one. I was nine and in that year some
woman from the town came and put her in a home where people with
tuberculosis went. They told us not to visit, but that didn't stop me and
my little sister Chi Chi, my big brother Eliseo and my two little brothers
Natali and Franklin. Every day, we walked the ten blocks and peeked in the
doorway at the room filled with sick people, watched as Mama laid in a bed
near the door and listened to her struggle to breathe; sounded like a whir
in the wind. When we called, she'd sit up and stare blankly at our skirts,
trying to figure out if it was really us or the ghost of someone that had
passed. Then she lifted her eyes to look at our pigtails and the boys' matted
hair. When we got closer, she'd kiss us, tell us to go home, that she'd be
there soon.

Our fathers never came, and no one watched us anymore. We did what we
had to, beg for food on the Avenida Sonrisa, sit near women in the town
square and go deep into their bags for colorful money. When we had it, I
cooked rice, boiled it in the iron pot my mother hadn't sold yet, ate with
our fingers the way she did. But mostly we lived on cans of beans that my
oldest brother Eliseo stole from the market and what the birds didn't find
on the Avenida Sonrisa. That was all we did for that month till the rent was
due and the landlord ended it. Mama ended it too. On the same day that the
landlord nailed a heavy lock on our door, and we brought Mama the last

of the rice, we stuck our heads in the doorway and didn't hear that whir anymore. Only beds upon beds of other people. People reading or coughing or lying still thinking of some far-off place where they would go when they closed their eyes for good. I like to think Mama went to some nice far-off place where she'd be thirty-one and beautiful and dancing forever. And where there wouldn't be no landlords.

We just kept on this way, sleeping near the fountain in the town square. Every day the boys went into the woods to find food but never did. And me and Chi Chi sat on a bench by the fountain and put on a sad face for the people who strolled by. One day, when the boys returned, they brought back yellow flowers. Then my little brothers Natali and Franklin started in.

"We saw Mama today," Franklin said, a week after we'd been living by the fountain.

"Mama gave us the flowers to give to you girls, they're sun flowers," Natali said.

The two of them stood in front of me without their shirts on, their little brown fingers gripped the flowers like they were holding spears. Soon they would accidentally break them, and I would cry if that happened. I snatched the flowers away and held them to my chest, rocking them like a baby.

"You saw her?" I asked. "Where, Natali?"

"In the woods."

I closed my eyes and brought the flowers to my nose. They smelled like wild cotton and of any type of juice. I put my lips on them, nibbled on the grainy dark spot in the middle.

"Why do you have to lie," Eliseo said. "If Mama was really around, she'd beat the two of you for lying." Eliseo stared them down, biting his mustache that had started to grow in since Mama died.

"And she'd beat you for stealing," Franklin started to cry.

"And she'd beat you for being half Jamaican," Eliseo said.

"I'm not Jamaican."

"Well, your father is."

From the town square I could see the ocean, and I could also see where our town ended and another one began. Beyond that — trees and then the jungle. A fog had begun to roll in above the trees and it spread through the town like a cloud of powder. Eliseo and the boys hadn't seen it, but me and Chi Chi did, and I looked right at it as it got closer. It crept up fast bringing the scent of the ocean and the jungle. The smell of swamps from the jungle and the sweet smell of sand from the beach. The fog covered us in no time and then rain started. Quickly, we gathered our bags and our money and the flowers so that we could find shelter below a tree nearby, but just as we did Eliseo passed out.

***

We found a house deep in the woods left behind by somebody who lived far away and didn't care who stayed there anymore. It was barely standing, broken steps — rotting, leading to the empty bedrooms upstairs. Walls that seemed to have been knocked down by a flood. We just all found a place on the floor and slept, and slept, for hours. And when we weren't sleeping, we were crying, and when we weren't doing that, we were reassuring each other that we could stay there for a long time. But when the rain and the wind and the bugs shot in through the broken windows, and when the jaguars came into our yard, we knew we couldn't live like this forever.

I told Chi Chi, "Listen, girl. If you cry too loud, they'll hear us and then your daddy will come get you. But I'll be left behind because my daddy would never come for me."

And Chi Chi, six years old, would open her big eyes and shake her head, bury her face in my hands. And that was enough to hush her for a while.

We didn't last but a few days in that house before a woman from the church came, riding a spotted horse and asking if we were the children of Maria Castellano, the black Colombian woman dancer. And Chi Chi said, "Yes." And the lady took out things from her bag. All the things that belonged to my mother: her headwrap and her perfume; her sandals, the ones she danced in; all the things my mother had brought with her to the place where she died. And the lady also had another bag that was filled with cans of beans. When we saw this, we laughed. She was a broad-shouldered, wheat-colored woman, like an angel. And we jumped in front of her and kissed her on her knees. She said, "The thing I remember is her voice. A shame she's not here. Her voice was magic."

A few days later she came again with more food and more water. And she said, "I'm looking for your fathers, tell me your surnames." And Eliseo said *Brimley*. And Chi Chi said, *Martinez*. And the two little boys of seven and eight, Natali and Franklin said, *Borbua*, because they had the same father. And when she got to me, I didn't know who my father was. She looked at me and said, "You don't know who your father is? But you look just like a Downer. You are a Downer, girl. I'll find him."

Because of this broad-shouldered woman, whose name I can't remember now, for almost a week we lived like kings, and we would wear Mama's clothes any chance we got, fighting over who would use her sandals or put on her wooden bracelets, the ones she wore to her shows. And we found pieces of dense wood that had broken off a fence, and knocked them against each other to hit a tune, dance like Mama taught us to dance in that African tribal way. And we sang in Igbo and in Spanish and yelled her name, our voices rising desperately into the sky. We were a sight. And when the jaguars came, they saw us and ran back into the jungle.

Soon, Mama wasn't the only one that went. The two little boys lay down in corners and stayed there day and night. Brave boys, telling me they were okay, that they just needed sleep to feel better again. When the broad-shouldered woman returned, she put their bodies on the back of a wagon and brought them into the woods; told us to stay put in the house until she got back. But as soon as she was gone, the three of us went outside, saw the black smoke rising over the jungle. It rose quickly like shooting pillars, unfazed by the wind and the trees, and even the birds that flew by, flew around it.

When the broad-shouldered woman got back from the woods, she handed me her handkerchief so that I could wipe my face of my tears. I would never again see my brothers, only in dreams, and only faintly when I looked at myself in a broken window of our new house and tried to smile.

The broad-shouldered woman let us ride her horse and I stopped crying for a while. Chi Chi sat in front of the woman and I sat in the back. We held onto her as she steered the horse. Eliseo stayed in the house watching from one of the windows in the living room as we made slow circles in the yard. We must have been squeezing the broad-shouldered woman because she kept rubbing my hand every time I tried to get closer to her. She said, "There are other children to feed. You're not the only ones. If I'm not busy, you'll see me again soon. I'll come back."

Dying feels like the skeleton of a kingfish in your neck. After my oldest brother Eliseo died, me and Chi Chi pushed his body across the living room floor and into the front yard. It had been only a few days since the others had passed, and we no longer had the strength or the need to dance. We just hummed the tunes now, forgetting some parts of them and feeling disgusted when we did. And when we finally remembered, we tapped into a place in us that felt amazing.

We laid our brother's body near a tree in the yard, the grass was wet from the rain that had fallen earlier and mosquitoes buzzed in our ears. Quietly, we said our goodbye to Eliseo. He wasn't sleeping when he went, he had died with his eyes open. He had taken every single moment, brave too like the rest of them. Or was it that just before he died, he had seen the others in the room, naked and jumping — full of breath, calling him to once again be closer.

When Chi Chi couldn't close Eliseo's eyes, we turned him over on his stomach. I wished so much that the broad-shouldered woman would come to take him away. She hadn't visited us since Natali and Franklin, and we wondered what had happened. It was normal for people to help needy children in Bocas. There were always hundreds of us wandering the streets, picking at the dirt like abandoned puppies. An adult or the church or the saints in the town would find a way to help, even though they themselves were poor. But I needed the broad-shouldered woman now more than the rest of them did. I feared the jungle, the blackness of it, the night bringing sounds that were louder than in the day; but I knew no one would come for us at this time of night. We would have to wait until morning to even have a chance of someone coming. Only a crazy person would travel in that darkness, and I feared that too.

Despite this, I had to say a final goodbye to Eliseo and go just past the clearing to get the leaves we needed to cover him, giant banana leaves that would hide us when we played in the yard and didn't want to be found. I grabbed Chi Chi's hand and went to where a family of banana trees were; and I began to pull their leaves, feeling their fluids drip down the sides of my arms and down my back. As we did this, the noises around us deepened and quickened, forming an echo in the canopy above us like the inside of a cave. And as we got further, just a few steps further, some of the noises stopped, then grew louder and faster yards away. Suddenly, something appeared before us, its green eyes gleamed behind the brambles. I pretended it wasn't there but when I looked away, it had moved to meet my eyes. The light from the moon revealed its dark spots, and it lowered its head and shot its shoulders forward, waiting for us to move.

"There is a jaguar there in the woods Chi Chi, girl. But don't look, just walk back and we will be safe in the house."

But Chi Chi ran and for the first time in my life, I followed my little sister, watching the back of her head, her plaits rising like tattered reins that I pulled with my eyes. We ran over loose branches, pieces of broken fence, puddles of rainwater, never looking behind me because if I did, the darkness of the jungle would have made me lose consciousness.

I followed Chi Chi up the steps, and we hid in the closet of the farthest bedroom, but there was no door to shut us in. Rubber trees broke in the woods and the wind shifted our roof. In the closet, we coughed of tiredness and of pain; we held tightly together up against its wet walls that broke as we trembled. We listened for the jaguar and prayed for it to leave as it had before. But there was nothing to keep it from us; because it was my spirit that had called the jaguar. I had called it. I wanted the jaguar to take my throat and break it in two. But it had not just been the jaguar I called, if it had been lightning, I would've wanted it to strike this house while we were asleep and bury us in smoke.

At night if a jaguar was chasing something outside, we could feel its paws striking the ground from anywhere in the house; and even though we kept the front door shut, we feared that a jaguar would come in somehow, through a hole in the roof, or through some other part we had not known existed yet; entering from a golden room, a room of hell, that when I dared to look at it, would blind me.

Now we heard the jaguar running up the stairs, scraping the hardwood, going in and out of rooms, as if it had visited the house before, or even lived there. As if it had come to reclaim its home. Soon everything would once again belong to the jaguar, when it would swallow my face and make me disappear.

I heard it enter through the broken window downstairs falling on the shards of glass on the floor. It stunk of the swamps we'd seen on our hikes, of the broad-shouldered woman's horse she let us ride, and of the fluids we'd rub on our arms that we thought would give us relief from mosquitoes but never did. And when I told Chi Chi not to cry, she quieted and squeezed my stomach.

Soon the jaguar stood before us in the dark, moving its nose around us like a dog. It's body and tail shifted as if it didn't quite know what we were or who we were. No longer did I know either; no longer did I know the difference between this life and the next. What was light or what was dark, what tasted good or what was dangerous to eat. I buried my head onto Chi Chi's shoulder and felt the jaguar's wet tongue on my hair. I shivered, the jaguar's face touched mine, softly, without harm, yet I was weakened even more, locked in place as if its tongue had poisoned me.

"I can't move," I said to Chi Chi but no sound came out.

The rain fell harder now, and I could hear it landing on the empty cans

we left in the other room. Even though my eyes were closed, I could still
see lightning; lighter and darker shades flashed in my shut eye followed
by thunder that scared me even before it broke. I got up to run, but when
I opened my eyes, the jaguar was gone. I heard it again in the other room
as it jumped through the glass of one of the windows on the second floor.
When it landed, the sound could be heard anywhere, even on Avenida
Sonrisa, and they'd know where we were and come for us, because we
couldn't scream. Still I wondered if someone would really come. I wanted
to trust in that, but what was trust? We were lucky, the jaguar had left us
alone. But I had no trust for anything or anyone. And it was not mercy
either that the jaguar had for us, because my brother had been enough for
it. The jaguar had eaten Eliseo. I did not have to witness it to know. But
me and Chi Chi held hands and walked slowly toward the window, careful
not to make a sound. We covered our mouths and stepped over the broken
glass; and when we got to the window, rain and wind came in, moving the
cobwebs on the walls.

It was a high window, and I could barely see anything. But I managed to
stand on one of the empty cans and look down. Chi Chi stayed close, but
the window was too tall for her.

"Is it still there?" she asked.

"Yes," I said.

"And Eliseo?"

I did not answer her. I held on to the windowsill and put my head outside,
careful not to touch the cobwebs. Eliseo was in another part of the yard
now, dimmer there near the brambles where we had picked the banana
leaves. He was turned on his side. His stomach was burst open, his feet and
legs moved side to side as the jaguar tugged at his skin and small organs.

The rain fell harder now, and the water began to spread over the yard making little ripples in it like a lake. I wished that I could look into the jaguar's eyes and make it stop, but I could only look at Eliseo and wonder what type of father he would've been because he was such a good brother.

The jaguar had not touched Eliseo's face. I could see his bronze skin, his plump cheeks and his eyes, the face of a handsome doll. Just before the jaguar left, it raised its long tail curving only the very tip. Then suddenly it turned its face to the jungle, its nose pointing at something nearby. Quickly, it shot its tail to the ground then went to whatever was there.

That night we held each other in the closet where we had seen the jaguar. Neither one of us slept. We decided that we would never go to the front part of the house. Always entering from the back. We never again said Eliseo's name, just referred to him as *my brother,* or *him,* or *the oldest.* And we prayed in the round blue night for the lady to come back for us.

Eventually, we didn't go outside at all. We just stayed in and slept upstairs, and we closed the door to the downstairs, which smelled awful, still fearing that the jaguar would return. But it never did. It left us alone. We didn't even feel its rumbles anymore when it chased things nearby. It left us alone now. Just like Mama did. They just all wanted us to be alone. Even God wanted that. Or was it that tuberculosis took the jaguars too? One by one it took the jaguars. It took our broad-shouldered woman away. It took our daddies away, and one day it would take our fight away too.

Lobo

by Deborah Leipziger

For Paulo Paulino Guajajara, known as "Lobo," Guardian of the Amazon, killed by illegal loggers

I guard the forest
its canopy of reflected stars
the morpho butterflies   the blue moons
bromeliads   the fish
the roots of trees
    drinking in the river

I guard the forest
the children of the tribe

I guard the canopy with its toucans   parakeets
emerald
I guard the forest floor   with its snakes
I guard the mating jaguars

I knew
they would kill me.
I could not have imagined
that it would be a shot to the
face   that my body would be
left in the forest

Now
You guard the forest

its canopy of reflected stars
the morpho butterflies   the blue moons
bromeliads   the fish
the roots of trees
    drinking in the river

You guard the forest
the children of the tribe

You guard the canopy with its toucans   parakeets
emerald
You guard the forest floor   with its snakes
You guard the mating jaguars

Fledged

by Diana Renn

The handoff took place at noon, inside our dim garage. Our neighbors, tense and talking fast, were in a hurry to get out of town.

They thrust the case of supplies at me. A syringe. A rubber heating pad. A bag of dog kibble. A container of crumbled hard-boiled egg and moist kibble. And then, to my son Gabe, they handed over the stainless steel bowl containing the baby bird.

It sat in a tangle of dried sphagnum moss commonly used for orchid-growing, which is one of our neighbor's more conventional hobbies. It lifted its black head and blinked sleepily, as the family, talking over one another, rattled off instructions for caring for the wild bird they'd rescued. Feed the bird every ninety minutes, sunup to sundown but not overnight. Remove poop from the nest by hand; the bird defecates as soon as it eats. Mash the dog kibble and egg very small. Place bits into the gaping beak until the bird stops chirping. Tweezers or a syringe could work; otherwise, fingers would do. No water, though — the bird could drown.

I stared warily at our new houseguest. A few days ago it had been almost covered in white downy fluff, and much smaller. It had looked helpless in its makeshift nest. Now, with more dark, mottled feathers sprouted, and a white tufted Mohawk, it looked less like a fuzzy alien and more like an actual bird. What kind of bird, none of us knew. What I did know was that caring for this bird for a week would be harder than we thought.

The bird had not had a great start in the world. It had fallen twenty feet from a nest on a floodlight outside our neighbors' house. They went up a ladder and replaced the bird. It tumbled out again the next day. Assuming it was injured or rejected, or both, the neighbors' teenage daughter had brought it inside their house, safe from predators. She'd been hand-feeding it diligently, her dad pitching in as needed. But then their family had the opportunity for a beach house rental on Cape Cod, a rare treat in a pandemic summer. That's why they had thought of the next best people to take over on short notice: my animal-loving son, and me, to supervise. Besides, we were already babysitting their chickens in their absence.

"So, um . . . what's the long-term plan?" I faltered, while my son made cooing noises at the bird. "I was reading online, you can't keep a wild bird in your house without a license. Maybe this should go to a wildlife rehabber."

My neighbors agreed. They'd tried to find one. But it turns out, wildlife rehabbers are a bit like unicorns, especially approaching the Fourth of July weekend. Especially during a pandemic when lots of places are closed. Even in normal times, there are not many rehabbers listed on the U.S. Fish and Wildlife website who will take in songbirds. Most of those listed have specialties like raptors or bats. Almost all rehabbers are at capacity and only take in clearly injured birds.

This bird looked pretty vigorous, shifting around in the moss. The slight upturn of its beak seemed like a smirk.

"Do you think it might want to fly soon?" I asked.

"If it does, you could just build it a little outdoor structure for it to move around in," my neighbor suggested. "With some wood and mesh."

I blinked. *Ah. Sure. Let me just gather some wood and mesh and build something. In between the hourly feedings from sunup to sundown. No problem. I'll just stay tethered to your bird all week. You guys go have fun at the beach.*

Gushing thank-yous, backing hurriedly out of our driveway, the neighbors headed off for vacation. Their car zoomed away.

Gabe and I brought the bird and supplies upstairs to the guest room. I closed the door firmly to keep out the cat. How had I let myself get strong-armed into this complicated caregiving situation? Why did people always think that just because I worked from home — even before Covid days — I was available to look after their plants, their chickens, their children, their dogs, their wild birds that have fallen from nests?

Gabe set up a card table in a dim corner. Grown birds flitted in the treetop outside the window, freely making their way to and from our feeders. Our little guest cocked its head. I closed the window and lowered the shade so it wouldn't be jealous.

The bird closed first one eye, then the other, settling in for a nap.

As I watched Gabe fuss with the bird's guest accommodations, I marveled at his lengthening limbs, the new angles in his face. He'd reached the edge of adolescence, having recently turned thirteen, and suddenly seemed so capable, as he plugged in the heating pad and placed the bird bowl on top. He arranged the food and feeding supplies, including tweezers and toothpicks if the syringe didn't work. Maybe this was a good project for him. Covid had canceled his normal summer plans. Maybe it was a good project for me, too. Saving one small thing, after so much loss in the world, had a distinct appeal.

We watched the bird breathe.

My breath caught in my throat. Suddenly this creature seemed so very fragile. Our caregiving efforts could fail. Or nature could take its course, and the bird would die on our watch. I didn't think I could handle one more sad outcome. Tears burned. But I blinked them away. *Don't bond with the bird,* I instructed myself. *We have to get it into more capable hands.*

Speaking softly while the bird snoozed, I showed Gabe the Massachusetts Department of Wildlife website. "Rehabbing birds is a delicate thing," I explained. "We're not trained. And this site says not to feed baby birds or bring them into your house. Our neighbors meant well, but this is like kidnapping. It's against the law."

His eyes widened. "Will we be arrested?"

"Well, probably not," I admitted. It was hard to picture U.S. Fish and Wildlife agents showing up at our door. Still, I like to think of myself as a law-abiding citizen.

Gabe nodded, taking this in. "We should keep trying to find a rehabber," he said quietly. "I mean, I want to keep it, but I know we should do whatever's best for the bird."

I hugged him. "Great. I'll keep calling around."

We didn't have time to discuss it further. The bird gaped its yellow beak and chirped urgently.

"Oh my God! It's hungry! Get the food!" I cried, helplessly waving my hands around.

Gabe calmly took tiny crumbles of moistened dog food and egg and dropped them into the yellow beak. The bird ate several drops of food, then wiggled and pooped. Gabe unflinchingly scooped the poop out and threw it away. He tenderly fluffed the moss around the bird.

The bird closed its eyes and went back to sleep. The soft breeze from the air-conditioning stirred its feathers and down.

My son's chest puffed a little. "See? This is easy."

"Ten feedings a day until we can turn it over to a rehabber," I reminded him. "I might not be able to get anyone until Monday. That's two whole days away. That's twenty feedings."

"Mom. I can do this."

"Okay," I said. I chewed my lip. "But I still think we need advice or help sooner." And suddenly, I knew just whom to call.

***

Somewhere deep in the woods not far from our house lives renowned bird artist and expert David Sibley. His field guides to birds are among the most revered books for birders. His illustrations are scientifically detailed works of art; we have identified all of our regular backyard visitors thanks to Sibley's work. Gabe and I looked through one of his most recent guides, and guessed that we might have a robin.

If I stumbled down enough side roads I might have found David Sibley eventually. He's an almost-neighbor who I know is out there: not visible but in calling distance, like a red-tailed hawk, or an eagle. He swoops in and leaves autographed copies of his books in our local bookstore, but I've never heard of local friends boasting they had a Sibley sighting at the local market. He's a low-profile celebrity, well-known to serious birders and probably amateur birdwatchers like us. Anyway, I was briefly tempted to track him down and leave our baby bird at his front door, like a foundling. To ring the bell and run. Much like I wanted to leave my infant son with the renowned sleep expert Richard Ferber in a nearby town, when the effort to sleep train felt overwhelming.

But finding David Sibley and begging him to take over was not a practical plan. Instead, I sought out the closest approximation I could think of: Greg, a young man in our neighborhood who had studied ornithology in college. He was now in graduate school. Covid had closed down his campus last spring. So he was living — like many twentysomethings I know — back in the nest, quarantining with parents.

His mother gave me his phone number. Greg was actually back in the lab for his graduate program this week, but would happily be on call for our project.

I texted Greg the photos of the makeshift nest on the heating pad, and told him about the feeding schedule. Greg confirmed the setup was perfect, though we might need to feed a bit more often — maybe more like every forty-five minutes. Twice as often as our neighbors had instructed us.

Oh. Okay. We'll just feed it every forty-five minutes. No problem. An image flashed into my mind: our unencumbered neighbors frolicking in the waves on a Chatham beach.

Greg also confirmed our suspicion from the Sibley guide, and identified the bird as an American robin. He texted a link to an infographic with a two-week growth model. The proportion of feathers to down suggested that the robin was eleven or twelve days old.

They leave the nest at day thirteen or fourteen.

This was welcome news. We'd simply open the window and let it go! Assuming the bird was uninjured, our problem would soon be solved.

But Greg's next text message caused a fresh surge of anxiety.

So what is the plan, post-fledging?

Plan? I texted back. *What do you mean?*

A fledgling bird, it turns out, is an avian adolescent. And just as we don't send thirteen-year-olds into the world to fend for themselves, robin parents continue to feed the baby for a couple of weeks after fledging. Not only that, fledglings do not return to the nest once they leave it. They move to a new, nearby roost with the parents. They hop around and gradually learn to use their wings and fly, which can take up to a week. In a month, they become proficient flyers with full-grown wings. Meanwhile, the parents — usually the dads — feed them and teach them valuable social skills, including how to identify bird calls that are critical to their survival.

I felt the floor fall away. Suddenly feeding by hand twenty times a day sounded relatively easy. *Fledgling* care was a whole different level of hard. I spent the next hour frantically googling. I read some rare accounts of people who'd raised fledglings and released them, with limited success after days of devoted care.

Just feed it some mealworms if you can't find real ones, but cutting up some real earthworms is better. Be sure to crush the mealworm heads. Just put out some bugs in dishes and teach it to feed itself. Just teach it to forage. Just continue to make sure it's eating a couple of times an hour since it's spending a lot of energy growing its wings and muscles.

The bird shifted in its bowl, startling me out of my research. It half-stood for a moment, then settled back down. It gaped for food and chirped. We were not yet at the forty-five minute mark, but it was clearly hungry. This job was definitely outside our pay grade. Fingers fumbling, I texted my on-call ornithologist once more.

So what are the signs it's getting ready to fledge?

Hopping, Greg texted back. *Moving its wings a lot. Getting in and out of the bowl. I take it you're keeping it outside?*

No. Inside. Guest room.

Pause.

Oh OK. Good, he wrote. *That way when it starts to fly, you'll be able to find it.*

I should have been relieved he wasn't reporting us to the authorities for keeping it inside. But I was now more anxious. This bird was going to have a whole different set of needs very soon. And this realization reminded me of times when I'd suddenly noticed my baby boy was more toddler than baby, outgrowing the car seat or the bouncy chair, and I hadn't yet bought the next wave of gear or finished childproofing the house. Or that sudden shock of clothes not fitting. A beloved toy no longer serving its purpose. That feeling of *wait, wait — I'm not ready!* — followed by rapid preparations, and settling into the next phase, adapting to new needs, providing for my child in a whole new way.

The bird's track record for leaping wasn't great, so Gabe and I laid blankets and towels on the floor in case the bird should try to launch from the card table. But my heart felt heavy. I knew full well we could not possibly provide for a fledgling, filling in for what its parents would be doing in the wild. There was even a danger the bird would imprint on us and no longer recognize its own kind.

We hadn't just taken in a baby bird. We'd taken in a teen bird.

And a problem.

***

Our neighbors were right. No wildlife rehabbers were answering phones on the Fourth of July, and the Tufts Wildlife Clinic — the most reputable operation in our area — was closed.

Late in the afternoon, Gabe and I went to the neighbors' yard to feed chickens and to inspect the original nest. We wanted to see how the siblings were doing.

More internet research indicated we could rig a nest close to the original nest, if the parents were still in the picture, and they might take over the feeding. Our neighbors had missed that chance, understandably assuming the bird was being rejected. I'm sure we would have assumed the same.

But robins, it turns out, are vigilant, hard-working parents. They might have three broods in a season, but only about 40% of their eggs will hatch, and only 25% of their fledged offspring will survive until the fall. Yet robin parents will do all they can to maximize every chance of success. If the bird is alive and visible, the parents will likely continue to care for it.

If this particular robin's parents had done anything wrong, it wasn't due to neglect. It was more likely a bad real estate situation. The nest was perched precariously atop the floodlight, over twenty feet off the ground, with no ledge and no barriers around it, and not even a tree to break a fall. Probably the birds had grown and filled the nest, and our bird had fallen. Twice. Replacing the bird a third time could cause even more harm and scare the siblings, Greg cautioned. We could see the two siblings, their yellow beaks open, their growing bodies filling the nest to capacity.

Suddenly, a shadow passed overhead. Gabe and I stepped back, observing in awe as an adult robin swooped in and fed the siblings. Back and forth it went, worms dangling from its beak, while the two birds in the nest twittered with excitement. Another adult robin looked on from a nearby tree. This family was still functional. We just happened to have the missing piece.

We ran back to our house and got the bird bowl. We put it on a short stepladder beneath the original nest.

"There's your baby! Feed your baby!" we coaxed the adult robin when it swooped by for the next feeding, a mere twenty minutes later.

The parent continued to swoop in and out, ignoring the chirping bird, focusing on the siblings. We let it go hungry for one feeding, waiting and hoping, before Gabe fed it mashed dog food himself and we brought it back to our house. "Maybe the neighbors were right," said Gabe. "This bird's parents didn't want it."

***

Sundown — and an end to the frequent feedings — couldn't come fast enough. I lowered the shade. I tiptoed backwards out of the room, as I used to do when Gabe was a baby, mindful of every floor creak that could wake my light sleeper.

Our neighbors had said to just start feeding the bird whenever we got up in the morning. But I set my alarm for 5:30. We'd seen such frequent feedings of the siblings that afternoon, I knew the bird would be hungry. I volunteered for the first two shifts, and Gabe promised he'd do the rest.

Very early the next morning, I paused with my hand on the doorknob. The room seemed eerily quiet. I dreaded opening the door. Much as I wanted relief from this growing problem we had on our hands, I didn't want to bury a bird. I suddenly had a profound fear that the bird didn't make it through the night.

Life felt so fragile, even precarious, lately. Hundreds of thousands of people were dying of this virus, often with little warning. People without the virus died abruptly, too. A dear friend of mine had quite suddenly lost her son. Her handsome, healthy, twenty-six-year-old adult child came home in March, along with her other two grown children, to quarantine in the family home. In June, he had a sudden health issue. He held on to life for a week, then passed.

My friend and her husband were excellent parents, the family extremely close-knit. They'd provided for their children, educated them, and done all the right things. During a public health crisis, they'd taken them all back in to keep everybody safe. That a random tragedy could strike this way simply made no sense.

I grieved with my friend every day. I wanted to help her. I could not do more than reach out by email and send a condolence card. Covid, cruelly, made a memorial service impossible. It also took away the basic comforts I could provide. I could not sit with her, hug her, or help her with household tasks. I did not want to burden her with obligations to reply to my check-ins, either. At the same time, I did not want to leave her alone in her grief. All I could do was send brief, occasional emails and texts, like bird calls: *I am here for you. I am here. I am here.* I rarely heard a response. It was as if my friend had vanished into dark woods, into a grief so deep I could not find her.

Standing with my hand on the guest room doorknob, unable to open that door, I worried my caregiving inclinations might inadvertently harm. I might have overfed the bird. I might have shined the light of the world too brightly at a grieving friend who wasn't yet ready to face it. How best to approach someone in a fragile state, someone whose world has been upended — whether because they've fallen, or because their baby has? How much to intervene? Why couldn't I back off and let things be?

I could always tell myself stories to justify my efforts. *The bird was abandoned. The friend wants comfort.* But the stories had more to do with me. With my own fear of change and loss.

I turned the knob. I opened the door. I opened my eyes.

The bird chirped. Its yellow beak opened wide as it saw me and clamored for food. My heart pounding, I hurried to it with my freshly prepared egg-and-kibble food, and fed it. Half the food dropped into the nest; I lacked my son's nimble dexterity. But some got in, and eventually the bird pooped and settled into the nest again, apparently satisfied.

So was I. I hadn't failed this bird. It survived the night, and I brought it some comfort.

As I wiped the table, something white caught my eye. Bird poop. Not in the bowl, but outside of it, on the heating pad, a few inches away. This bird had at some point hopped out of the bowl and gotten back in.

We had even less time than I had thought.

Which is true not just of birds, I suppose, but of life itself.

***

After two more bird feedings and a human breakfast (skipping our own usual fare of scrambled eggs, which suddenly lacked appeal), Gabe and I made a decision. We would take the bird back to its original home to keep an eye on the siblings. If our bird was ready to fledge, the siblings would be too. They could fledge together. They could be reunited on the ground, and the parents could take over.

We took the bird bowl and carried it to our neighbors' yard, slowly and carefully, until a giant hornet pursued us and we had to pick up the pace.

In our neighbors' yard, still shaking from the close brush with the hornet, we put the bowl on the small step stool beneath the original nest and walked back about ten feet.

The fledgling looked around, a soft breeze rifling the last little tufts of white down that poked up through dark feathers. His breast was more spotted now, and faintly brownish red. Was he looking for us? For me — his mom now? I swallowed hard. It was hard to ignore those plaintive peeps. But if we continued to hover too close, the real parents would not approach.

There was a lot of rustling and chirping going on in the original nest far above him. Excitement in the air.

While we waited for a parent, I worked the phone. If Operation Robin Reunion failed, this bird had to leave our house. We could not care for the bird once it fledged.

I finally reached someone at the Massachusetts Audubon Society. She informed me, in a clipped tone, that they do not take in birds, and, furthermore, it's against the law to have a wild bird in your home. "It needs to go to a rehabber," the woman informed me. She suggested the same websites I'd already looked at. "But we've all done it," she added, in a softer tone. "We've all taken in a helpless robin and tried to do our best for it. Unfortunately, it usually doesn't work out the way we hoped. I wish you all the luck with your bird."

The sun burned hotter. The robin parents had not yet appeared. Had something happened to them?

The vibrating phone in my hand startled me; I nearly dropped it. "H-hello?"

"This is the Tufts Wildlife Clinic. We got your message. About the bird."

Relief coursed through my veins. Tufts! Surely they would help.

I told them all about the bird. My temporary joy ebbed when the administrator confirmed that rehabbers for songbirds were hard to find, and that their clinic only took in injured birds. Our bird didn't sound injured. "If you truly can't find anyone, you can bring it here," she relented. "But we're likely to euthanize it even if it's healthy, if no one can take it in." She proceeded to give instructions on how to place the bird in a box for transportation.

I ended the call with a heavy heart. Someone would take the bird off our hands. That was what I wanted. Right? This was the best possible outcome of a bad situation. But after all this valiant effort, somehow it didn't feel right.

"I don't think the parents are coming," Gabe said with a sigh. He fed it a bit more dog kibble, then backed away again.

The bird still seemed restless, not inclined to nap as it usually would after eating. It was moving. Moving a lot.

Suddenly the bird jumped out of the bowl.

Gabe and I rushed to it, arms outstretched.

The bird shook its feathers and lifted its head. Then it leaped onto the ground, eluding us.

Gabe and I dropped to the ground as well.

It hobbled a bit, then began to hop. Slowly, at first, then faster, changing directions. On sturdy legs.

We followed on hands and knees, still keeping a careful distance, but not daring to let it out of our sight.

The robin parents returned, one of them feeding the siblings in the nest above, ignoring the lost baby on the ground.

"Maybe he fledged too soon," I whispered.

"But he's so strong," Gabe whispered back. "Oh, no! Come back!" he then cried, as the bird headed into a blueberry bush, away from the nest area, out of the sightlines of the flying parents.

Gabe got up and ran in that direction. He followed the bird into the bushes. I started to protest — *don't scare him!* — but bit my tongue.

Moments later, he emerged with the flapping bird in his hands. He carried it gently to the middle of the lawn, directly beneath the parents' flight pattern to and from the nest. "They need to see him," he said.

The fledgling looked so tiny and lost in that vast expanse of lawn. I hardly dared to look away in case I lost sight of the speck of dark brown.

Back and forth the parents swooped, feeding the two siblings still in the nest.

Our bird, softly, then more insistently, began to chirp.

An airplane roared overhead, drowning out its pleas.

I buried my face in my hands. Having an adult bird see or hear the fledgling, and connect with it, seemed as remote a possibility as the SpaceX shuttle docking with the international space station, a miracle of precision planning and timing and some degree of luck.

And yet, that miracle had indeed happened a few weeks before. Why not hold on to hope that these birds, too, would align?

The plane passed. The fledgling continued to chirp, louder now, insistent. *I am here. I am here. I am here.*

I looked up again. A shadow fell on the ground.

A bird. A large, dark robin. One of the parents.

It landed on the lawn about ten feet from the fledgling, tilting its head.

Gabe and I clutched each other's arms and watched, hardly daring to breathe.

The adult robin ducked its head and pulled a worm from the earth. It hopped to the peeping fledgling. Closer. Closer.

The fledgling hopped to the adult. It gaped its beak.

The adult robin ducked its head almost entirely into the fledgling's beak and fed it the entire worm.

I texted Greg, my fingers shaking. *It's happening!* I snapped a picture of the next worm-insertion, as proof.

His response came fast. *That's amazing!*

The parent found several more worms, which the fledgling eagerly consumed, twittering with excitement between each feeding. Then the parent flew off, and the fledgling hopped to a shady patch of daylilies and settled into the grass. I also sent pictures of the whole sequence to our neighbors who interrupted their Cape Cod fun to respond with virtual cheers and smiley emojis.

I turned to Gabe. "Wasn't that incredible?"

He nodded, but scratched his bug bites. "Can I go back home now?"

I frowned. "You should stay and see this through," I said.

"I did. We're done. It worked," he said. "And all my friends are online."

So I let him go, watching his loping gait as he ran back across the street, eager to escape to the virtual world that enticed him. More and more I would be seeing this view of him. His back to me, running off. Fledging. Then flight.

I, the original reluctant foster bird parent, remained in the neighbors' backyard, rooted to the spot, baking in the sun. I felt morally incapable of leaving. Or emotionally incapable. I just wanted to be sure it wasn't just a one-off feeding, a pity handout, and that the parent bird was really going to take over.

I nodded off in a plastic chair, until a chirping bird woke me. The fledgling! It was back on the lawn, much farther than where we'd originally placed it. In the shade. Would the parents see it again?

I scanned the surrounding trees for signs of the adult robins. The trees were still. No birds sang. I followed the fledgling softly, the container of dog food in hand.

The fledgling gave me what felt like a passing glance, but its attention was elsewhere, scanning, looking for the real parent.

I held out a pinch of food. The bird paused. Then it peeped and hopped away from me. This was a good thing, I reminded myself. A bird imprinted on humans would not likely survive. But if the parents didn't appear again, what were its odds of survival?

I texted Greg an update. *So now what?*

Just keep your eye on it throughout the day, he texted back. *The parents should continue to feed it. The siblings should fledge soon. And then the parents should take everyone to a safe space for the night.*

What if they don't? I asked.

You can just try to catch it and take it inside again.

As I was contemplating how to recapture a fledged bird that no longer wanted my offerings, and the ethics of driving it to Tufts at this point, a rustling of wings startled me.

A parent was back, a worm in its beak. The fledgling hopped straight to it. Mealtime number two had commenced. I watched in rapt attention. Only after I saw the fledgling hop back to the daylilies, belly full, did I feel I could leave.

I returned to the yard multiple times throughout the day to check up on the robin family. When Gabe came with me on one check-up visit, he pointed to the nest and gasped. Bits of straw hung over the floodlights. No little brown heads or yellow beaks were visible.

Sometime during the day the siblings had fledged too. We'd missed the big event. But where were they? Our bird appeared to be the only one on the lawn, and still one of the parents kept watch, perching on nearby trees, then responding to its cries for food. Had the siblings survived the drop to the ground, and managed to hop to safety? Or had a hawk swooped in before they even had a chance?

I returned to the yard with binoculars and settled into the neighbors' treehouse, scanning for the siblings. No luck.

After dinner, I returned to the treehouse one last time, and could not find the siblings nor our fledgling. The sun was dipping low, turning the tops of the trees to gold, but clouds were fast approaching. My weather app warned of a storm. High winds, driving rain. If I were going to take it in for a night, this would be the time.

I scanned every tree ringing the lawn until I saw the fledgling. It was in a slender pine tree, about two feet off the ground. Already it had grown strong enough to flutter up and perch upon a branch. The new roost. The parents had found shelter.

The parent robin swooped on to the branch and fed it. I let out a long breath, and wished them well. I lowered the binoculars, climbed down from the treehouse, fed the chickens, and headed home.

***

That should have been the poetic end of the story. But in fact I spent much of the next several days camped out in the neighbors' yard with binoculars. Gabe went back to his friends and his video games, the novelty having worn off, his work complete. For him, the story had a happy ending: the bird returned to its parents. I felt compelled to continue to watch, to monitor, to hover. I caught glimpses of it at times, no longer on the lawn, but deeper in the woods, higher up in trees, still being fed. I was sure I heard other peeps as well, which I hoped were the siblings.

My world, already shrunk by the pandemic and our cloistered existence, shrunk even smaller to the size of what I could view through my binoculars. I couldn't leave this bird. I couldn't leave this story. I wanted the assurance of a happy ending. Even by the third day, when I couldn't see the birds at all — when I could only hear the distant birdsong in the woods — I trained my lenses on the thickets of trees, hoping for a flap of feathers, for a rush of motion. Okay, I'll admit it — for a nod of recognition. A lingering gaze as if to thank me. A real Disney ending.

None of that happened. The neighbors eventually returned from the Cape, a bit early, looking surprised — and, frankly, amused — to see me exiting their yard with my binoculars in hand, twigs and leaves hanging off my clothes and hair. That put an end to my frequent yard visits. The bird was not mine. I had to let go.

Still, in the weeks and months since then, I've stopped to look at every robin in our street, wondering if it is our fledgling, wishing I had some confirmation that it is thriving in the world. I would like to think that it is. Robins are amazing parents, persisting despite the slim odds of their eggs hatching, their babies fledging, their fledglings surviving.

And people are amazing parents too, as well as great launchers of beginnings. We launch children, stories, space shuttles, all kinds of hopeful endeavors into the world, despite not knowing the endings.

Despite efforts and good intentions, though, not all fledglings make it. Some fall, no matter how hard their parents try, no matter how much help is offered.

Reuniting the bird with its family felt satisfying, but did nothing to change my friend's situation, the loss of her beautiful boy. It did not restore any sense of balance to the universe. What it did do was help me better understand the reality of loss. Loss happens. It happens all the time. Sometimes there's simply nothing we can do. There's often no explanation.

Now the summer birds that remain are busy, eating and getting stronger, preparing for fall migrations. Flocks of birds startle me lately, with their sudden movements and sounds and their exquisite beauty. So fragile yet so strong. I take time to watch them in a way I never did before.

Similarly, I watch older kids — high school and college kids, graduate students, all those in Generation Z who are flying a bit ahead of my son. Gabe will be flying in that V-formation with them in a scant few years. Where will they all be going? What kind of world will they enter? How will they confront this enduring virus, or climate change, or other dangers to come? Many of these fledglings reversed migration and came home; can they launch again? Have we taught them enough? Will they know where to find food, where to shelter, how to build, and our calls?

I am here. I am here. I am here.

Even though I don't know the final outcome for our bird fledgling's new life, I marvel at the incredible relay race we got to be a part of in its launch: from our good-Samaritan neighbors, to our young ornithologist friend, to the original bird parents, all of us passing the baton, sharing the load, trying to give it a shot.

If all we gave to the bird were opportunities for fresh worm meals, and sunlight, and a soft breeze in its feathers, and a safe perch in a pine, and the chance to grow and stretch its wings and learn to fly a little, even if just for a few days, then that is already a story with a happy ending.

Maybe that's what parenting is. We do the best that we can, in the time that we have, not knowing the end result.

Maybe that's what life is too. Appreciating all the happy endings we can find. Then releasing. Then letting them go.

In Defense of Trans Childhood

by Taylor Sprague

My childhood feels distant, far more distant than the number of years that span my lifetime. It belongs to another person, one I tried so hard to be because of the manual I was handed, the rulebook I was prescribed. I hold photos of myself between the tips of my fingers, trying not to smudge the images more than they already are in my mind. Long hair, pink Girl Power shirts, white dresses on Easter. Ballet classes, a sweet sixteen, an overly embellished prom dress. These are the artifacts I struggle to identify. I know they are a part of my past. What else could they be? And yet, they feel stolen. Stolen from me or by me, I'm not quite sure.

I don't talk about my childhood much because it does not belong to me. It belongs to the society that handed me a personality, a life, because I was born with the body parts that deemed certain traits necessary. Combing doll hair and painting nails. Blushing around boys and growing into heels. I got chastised once for wearing a men's belt at 21 years old, when I should have known better to choose feminine clothes. I don't know what that means for me now, my closet is filled with men's shirts and shoes and belts. It's not like those labels are correct, either. Just an array of ill-fitting garments that lie lifeless on a body striving to be alive.

When I do afford myself the opportunity to reflect on my childhood, the space between my rib cage swells with longing, the memory of asking for that which I could not have. Can I play football instead of being a cheerleader? Can I take woodshop instead of chorus? Can I have an action figure instead of a doll? Arriving at McDonald's for a Saturday afternoon lunch, the anticipation of a red cardboard box smiling back at me felt like microdosing Christmas morning. And yet, getting the "girl toy" was the easiest way to take the happy out of the meal, a disappointment I became so familiar with that hope started to taste like cheap wine. The hangover was never worth the buzz.

I remember trying desperately to make up for the sand that was slipping between my fingers by moving into my brother's room the moment he moved out. I was a junior in high school and considerably tired of the floral curtains that hung alongside purple walls and the menagerie of dolls staring down at me from floating shelves. I left the larger room with the built-in bookshelves and desk, fixtures my adult self pines for, to find solace in the dark blue walls and sports-inspired décor. It felt like trying on a life, hoping the change in scenery would change the hue of my spirit. I cannot say whether I slept better within those walls, but I remember feeling a little more at home. Or, at least, a little less out of place.

When I couldn't find boyhood on turf fields or in sawdust covered workshops, I searched for it at the bottom of bottles and on the street corner, just shy of school property, where the smokers gathered. In growing up, I burned childhood down to the roach of a joint clip, my sense of self becoming less of a priority the redder my eyes grew. I threw punches to make up for never learning to throw a fastball. I hurled insults because that was what I'd learned boys do. I broke spirits to make up for the fact that I was broken. Today, I stack my regrets next to the books that line my shelves, never forgetting that my own self-hatred made me the antagonist in someone else's story.

When I do revisit my childhood, I strive to find the constant — the things that have never changed in a life defined by transition. The way my voice speeds up when I get excited, the fullness in my chest when I walk through nature on the first warm day after a harsh winter, the fact that I tear up at the slightest hint of sentimentality. When I think back on that kid, writing in their bedroom or long-boarding down a suburban hill, I know who they are. They are me, albeit a bit lost. The moments I was alone are the moments I look back to with such familiarity, a deep understanding of who that child is and was. I take pride in the ways that I made space for myself, how I carved a place into this world where I could exist beyond external expectations. I try to remember there are more days ahead, ones where I can make my own choices, irrespective of what anyone might say I *should* do. But my memories are not all in isolation, and the context of my life is shaped by the people who have been a part of it.

When my family and friends revisit my past they trip over the memories, unsure of how to refer to me, aware that the language has changed but, perhaps, the person is the same. I reconnect with former teachers and family friends, those I've not seen since long before my transformation, and wonder if we will ever return to familiar ground. I watch them struggle with how to reminisce on simpler times. With just one word, a minority of 26 letters rearranged to form a new pronoun, the meaning of the memory rearranges like the beads of a kaleidoscope. The lens is the same, the image entirely unfamiliar. It shifts from a shared moment to a distant history, as if read from the pages of a textbook. Sterile, removed, lacking the sentimentality that makes one's heart swell.

It is for these reasons that my heart breaks for the transgender children of Texas, Idaho, red states with red-faced legislators spreading fear of their existence. My experience with transitioning has been alongside the growing conversation, among youth and adults, that trans people exist and have basic needs that small changes could fill. My confidence in the future grows every time I hear of a 12-year-old who feels strong enough to say, "call me they," or when I hear of children who cannot understand why cutting their hair or painting their nails should be considered brave. For authenticity to be second nature and for the language of their truth to be at arm's reach is progress of which we cannot fathom the lifetime impacts.

My heart swells for trans youth because I know that they will look back on their photos with pride. Their families will tell childhood stories with the correct pronouns because they have never been wrong, because they roll off the tongue. They will look back at their teenage years and, as they reflect on the inevitable mistakes we all make in our youth, know that their gender does not belong in the pile of regrets. Their prom will feel embarrassing and awkward because they had not grown into their limbs or figured out how to style their hair, not because it forced a smile in clothes that felt like a prison. They will have the chance to hold diplomas bearing the true name of the person who earned it. They will love and be loved and never question whether it didn't work out because they were looking at the wrong people, or they were the wrong person, all along.

To the people who would take this congruence away, who would rip self-determination from the hands of a child who damn well knows who they are, hear this. While you punish parents for what you call child abuse because they have the audacity to love their kid in all the ways they show up in the world, you are punishing children. You are punishing them for asking for help, for voicing their needs, for telling their parents the hardest truths they will ever have to share. You are punishing them for daring to claim their lives as early as they can, in hopes that more of their memories will feel like their own. You are punishing them for using their own hands to write their stories with the expectation that when they turn the pages, they are not turning away from a chapter they can never revisit.

When you tell trans children they are too young to know who they are, you create a lifetime of loss, the moments compounding until they, inevitably, still pursue the truth they've always known. Except the bridge required to connect childhood to adulthood will be longer, less sturdy, cracking in more places than can ever be deemed secure. But our infrastructure need not be crumbling. The potential for a history of heartbreak is entirely preventable. And the lives lost as collateral damage in your vendetta against a youth well spent need never be ended so soon.

And all it costs from you is to let children live, let parents love, and leave us to figure out the rest for ourselves.

valentines day

by Serina Gousby

this day
I wasn't in my body anymore.
spineless in the reflection
of widespread windows
barriers of glass doors
closing, needles and
beeping and jumpsuits
eyes and warm sheets.

I met many eyes
eyes made of sun
always there to see mine fog
they watered often
doors sliding and
water squeezing
coughing out air I couldn't keep in
liver failing of no pain
a mute peace I entered

I remembered boardwalks and
grass but not the type of grass you stomp on
but you float and
the rush of griot and collard greens seeped
in my nostrils and the warmth of shea butter
I thought of bricked steps and

echoes of laughs by the river and
guitar chords and penny loafers in reverse
    all the joys are erasing

didn't know how to say goodbye
maybe it wasn't time
just enough movement
of my fingertips to speak
all I could read were hearted emojis
scrolled and scrolled and scrolled and
forgot what a tight sealed hug felt like
this was enough, now.

I wanted this body to come back
this body I hated
ripped up and shredded with my words
the body I wasn't sure would fight for me
I didn't make myself proud yet
I hated the fiery burned nostril through
this tube and the tiredness of each hard breath
out and in, out and in, sudden movement
and coughing out of air and those eyes would come back
    they would always come back

I told them who I was
when joy made sense to reach after
the first time I felt free
walking across the bridge under the sun
above the water, water I missed

missing pencil ridges and lettered portraits
I told those eyes I never fell in love before
I let go of my phone
I wanted to stop.

every night I heard gospel
fist up, shaking
caressing the soul of my fingers
afraid to sleep out my lungs
my body hugged me just before 1am
      let me back in.

Man and Sky in Daytime

by CB Anderson

We are surrounded by curtains.
— René Magritte, 1929

I.

They had just returned from Paris, where things did not go well. There was the spider, yes, but the end came at a party when the host confronted Magritte's wife about her cross. The host was a painter too, with a larger and more vocal following than Magritte.

Georgette had gotten the cross for her twelfth birthday; the host suggested she remove it. The cross was small, 18 karat, smoothed from twenty years of wear. Magritte knew it as well as he knew the shade of Georgette's nipples and the twin moles on her back. He was not a religious man, but he was steadfast. He got up and she got up, and they left the table. Three days later they boarded the train for Belgium.

II.

The spider: early in their stay they'd gone for aperitifs with artists Magritte had met. The atmosphere felt both unrestrained and postured, and he wondered, not for the first time, whether so many outward gestures came at the expense of inner calm. He was in Paris to paint and to sell his work, and if his Belgian-Walloon accent embarrassed him, it did so only mildly. His mind was sifting through this when the man beside him reached into a pocket, pulled out a box, and placed a spider in his mouth. Chewed, swallowed. The expression on Georgette's face didn't change. She simply pushed her Kir to the center of the table and left it there.

Things had not gone well in Paris and still weren't good. It was July, 1930. At first Magritte had felt relieved to be home — the plain uncrowded streets, their apartment, summer warmth. It had rained almost every day in Paris. Georgette unpacked their belongings. She set about restocking the larder. Magritte sat at his easel in a corner of the dining room, the dog at his feet. He was having trouble painting. Each day he told Georgette about it, and each day she listened.

III.

The host's name was Frédéric, and Georgette had been capable of her own defense. Magritte knew this but got up from the table even so. He and Georgette had stayed with Frédéric when they first arrived in Paris. They'd brought their dog, a Pomeranian named Louis, with them. Frédéric sometimes bought bones for Louis from the boucherie around the corner.

Magritte's painting had gone well enough in Paris, but he'd sold only a few pieces.

IV.

At home, Georgette was not herself; the clatter from the kitchen seemed intentional. Their third day back she gathered Louis and went to market, red hair caught atop her head. Her father taught maths, her mother kept house. Georgette was not fond of psychological theories or fanciness of any sort. On weekends she worked as a night nurse. From the start she'd called him by his last name, and he liked that she did. At the end of the War, he'd returned from conscription knowing that he wanted to marry her.

V.

The silence made Magritte uneasy. He left his easel and put Satie on the gramophone, and when that induced nothing in him replaced it with Ravel, still to no effect. He stared out the window at the brick apartment building next door. He was working on a painting of a man but could not paint the face. When he was fourteen, his mother had drowned herself.

Georgette came home. She set out lunch. Five hours later she set out dinner. They talked some, but there wasn't much to it. Two more days passed this way. Only Louis was himself, jumping off the bed at dawn and rushing to the door that opened onto the garden. Every morning Magritte got up and let him out. Then he made coffee in their small kitchen, brought two cups back to bed. He and Georgette sat against their pillows and drank, uneasiness between them.

VI.

"Do you see me differently?" he asked, not sure what he meant.

She said, "Don't be silly."

"I'm having trouble painting."

"I know you are. You'll find your way."

"Are you still upset about the cross?"

"I'm not."

She opened her book of puzzles — she did one every morning. Magritte looked over her shoulder. He thought he might help.

"Magritte, please."

"Where were you yesterday in the afternoon?"

"At Veronique's. I brought her some cuttings."

He liked her friend Veronique, but not tremendously.

Georgette said, "I'm getting up."

As she did, her legs flashed like scissors, and Magritte felt himself get hard. He thought of them fucking and leaving the sheets in shreds.

VII.

At night he had dreams, and in the mornings he wrote them down. Some were about Georgette and sex but many weren't. He hadn't told anyone in Paris that he kept a journal. In it he mostly noted objects: oranges and locomotives, clouds and rocks, umbrellas. His father, a tailor, had taught him the importance of a well-made suit. Their fifth night back home, Magritte dreamed he was in a room with a birdcage. But instead of a bird, the cage held a large egg. Writing this down in the morning, he felt even more unsettled. Why the egg? And why had it seemed natural? He got up but could not work. The man's face still would not be painted. Georgette retrieved her shopping basket and whistled to Louis.

"We're off," she said. Her tone was pleasant. Magritte asked whether she might pick up meat pie for dinner.

In the dining room he finished a third cup of the coffee he'd made after letting Louis out — the good, chocolaty coffee they always bought. He'd missed it those months they were away. He selected a tube of white paint.

Uncorked the turpentine and sniffed. He stared at the faceless man, and the faceless man stared back.

VIII.

On the train home from Paris, they passed fields yellow-wet in the rain. There were thousand-year-old villages and younger ones with factories. Beside him Georgette dozed, eyes scrolling behind lids, as intent in sleep as when she was awake. A nursing manual lay open in her lap. In a clearing, men stood around the hood of a car, their backs to the train. Everything was backwards to the train — backyards, back doors, the backsides of women bending over vegetables. On their itinerary Magritte wrote: rooster, automobile, tomato. Doing so might prime his dreams, or it might not. He put a hand on Georgette's knee. The train pushed onward. He'd found Paris reassuringly recovered from the War but so sure of itself, externalized, the artists there expending their energies on eccentricity. Yet *le mouvement surréaliste* felt conformist, even orthodox.

IX.

The telephone rang, startling him. The mail — it came, mostly welcome, they read it when they wanted. The telephone intruded. Magritte hadn't wanted one, but Georgette did. He went into the kitchen and lifted the receiver.

"You're home." Bernard, his dealer.

"Since Sunday, yes."

Bernard got to it quickly — Magritte knew he would. "Your last series didn't sell as we'd hoped. Those figures in the forest. Too post-war grim."

Magritte twisted his wedding band. He did not remind Bernard that three of the paintings had sold to a well-off buyer from Greece, enough to pay six months' rent. He said, "I've got oils open, Bernard. I can't really talk. But you'll have the piece I've been working on soon."

After he hung up, he broke and buttered a baguette. His temples thrummed — the call or too much coffee or both. Maybe the bread would help. At his easel, he considered setting aside the faceless man and painting something he'd done before. Replicating it. The False Mirror? The Adulation of Space? Both were easily reproducible. He liked making copies of his earlier works, the feeling constant from one piece to the next. There was liberation in it — similar to the relief in an encore, the pressure of performance gone, only the music left. But Bernard did not approve of reproductions. And Bernard would call back soon.

X.

This came to Magritte about his dream: the egg had looked so natural because the cage paired with the bird, and the bird with the egg. And so, the egg with the cage. He went back and forth between disliking and liking products of the mind, including his own. He painted from his dreams, but a dream was indissectible. Understanding the egg and the cage belonged together was enough. He could paint that after he finished the man. But what should he do here?

Think with your eyes, he reminded himself. Eventually he set out dabs of white, blended in red until he had a half-dozen tints of pink. He began. A rounded shape appeared, scalloped on the edges. He started filling the interior. The brush felt good in his hand. He hummed a little. After a while the door clicked open and Louis trotted over. Magritte petted the dog's ears but kept painting. The object was developing. It was not a face.

Georgette set down the shopping basket. "Too hot out," she said. She leaned over him. He smelled lily *eau fraiche* and underarms. "What is that?" she asked.

"I'm not sure," he said. "A flower maybe."

She peered at it. "It looks a little strange. It looks — what did you paint when you worked in the wallpaper factory?"

"Cabbage roses."

"Yes, like one of those," she said.

XI.

Magritte had painted cabbage roses as a draughtsman at the factory, when they were first married. The wallpaper had been hand-drawn before it went to print.

"That doesn't really look like you," Georgette said again.

Magritte shrugged. His chest felt a little tight. He said, "I'm working here."

She straightened, "I hope it goes well." A pause. "We can have lunch in the garden."

"Alright," he said.

He blended cadmium yellow into one of the pinks and a coral hue came up. Petals took form. It was indeed a rose, and he was painting for the first time in days. Georgette was right, though. The rose was detailed — fine-stroked and three-dimensional — in a way that didn't look like him. He could practically smell the heavy scent. So be it.

"You are always who you are," his father had said the fourth or fifth time they moved houses after his mother was gone.

XII.

Wallpaper had helped put food on their table for those two years. He hadn't disliked painting cabbage roses. There was something in it. Sweat beaded his upper lip. He ran his tongue over it. Salt. He did not dream of his mother but thought someday he might.

Georgette called him to lunch. Magritte was glad to lay down his brush. Ordinarily his shapes were clean and crisp, thin on the canvas, but with every stroke the rose grew more ornate. In the garden she'd set out tuna nicoise. He felt too warm to eat. He poured a glass of water.

He said, "I can't say why I'm having so much trouble with that piece. I've looked for something from my journal, but nothing feels right. Maybe I'm not writing down enough in the mornings."

"I know you'll figure it out," she said.

They argued — Georgette complained that Louis was digging up the delphiniums and irises, and Magritte told her to fence them off. She said he should put up the fence, and after that he should separate the dictamnus. She said he'd told her he would do it last fall, before they left for Paris, and he never did. Magritte raised his voice: *"I'm busy."* Georgette smacked the table, hard enough to make the dishes jump, and Louis ran out from under it. She said, "We're both busy, Magritte. I need to sort the upstairs and iron my uniform for tomorrow. The boulangerie was out of your meat pie. What do you want to do for dinner?"

XIII.

Magritte didn't know. Shame flared inside him, as though Georgette working on the weekends indicted him, and he should be draughting wallpaper instead of painting. Was she funding an indulgence? He got up and cleared the table. Fear now, alongside the shame. He couldn't stand disharmony between them. Every time it came, he took her discontent as final. Inside the house he felt something close to frantic, and a need for motion. He yanked the shopping basket from its hook. He called, "I'm going out." Passing the easel, he was seized by an impulse. He pulled a palette knife and rag from his bin and scraped at the paint. In seconds the rose was gone. He wadded the rag and dropped it. He'd paint over the smear that remained when he got back.

On the street the heat pressed up against him. Magritte's steps were slow and hard. Good. By the time he reached the square, his shirt was wet.

XIV.

At the boulangerie, still no meat pie — he settled for a quiche. The fig tarts looked okay so he got four, and a liter of mineral water. Outside, crows squabbled in the hemlock that overhung the park. He drank the water while nearby two tourists photographed each other by the War memorial. The man posed first, then soberly they traded places. Afterward the woman lit a cigarette. Magritte reached into the basket and pulled out a tart. It was good. He ate another and left two. He considered offering to take a photo of the tourists together but did not. Watching them was cinema.

Two more stops: lettuce from the vegetable stall and a box of chocolates. He and Georgette could eat them and drink wine while they read in bed that night. They couldn't be unhappy with each other. He could not let that happen. All order and quietude in his life was due to Georgette.

XV.

It was cooler now, less humid. Magritte took the long way home, around the duck pond and across the vacant schoolyard. The basket rubbed against his thigh. He didn't shop often, but he liked it when he did. The feeling of bounty, of taking care of things. Georgette might tell him he'd done well, or she might not. It would be all right.

It came to him as he turned down their street. The man in the painting did not have a face — no human face, no rose, no apple, no object Magritte had ever written in his journal. There was nothing above the shoulders except sky and possibly a bowler hat. The piece would be different enough from the others he'd done. A title: "Man and Sky in Daytime." Magritte felt lighter. He'd finish it by Monday, and Bernard would have it by the end of the month. Georgette was in the dining room when he got home. He went to her and offered up the basket.

He said, "I understand what to do with the painting now."

XVI.

She glanced at what he'd brought. She said, "I'm happy you've figured it out."

Magritte sat at his easel, frowned at the smear. "I was trying too hard," he said. "Everything we see hides another thing. And what does it even mean, when finally all is mystery. Why try for explication?"

Georgette nodded.

He continued, "So you search for images and invent. The idea doesn't matter. Just what's on the canvas, and the mystery. That's the only way to paint."

"Well," she said, "it's good you know what you want to do." She picked up the basket, paused. "Does any of this need to go in the ice box?"

XVII.

"I try to find a solution to the problem every object poses," he told her. "Be it any object whatsoever—"

"Magritte, you're going on. You've been like this since Paris."

He stared at her.

"It's true," she said. "It happens every time your work stalls."

In Paris, Georgette had called Frédéric and the others *your friends*. She'd said Magritte wanted to be like them. But actually — he didn't know. He hadn't felt natural around them. Yet on rainy afternoons he'd liked to paint with the others under the café awning, and the spider hadn't upset him the way it did Georgette. Magritte understood this much: he and his work were the reason they'd been in Paris all those months. He wasn't sure he was very good, but it was what he did.

His eyes watered. He said, "While I was out, I thought how fortunate I am to have you."

His cheeks were horrifyingly wet, and her gray eyes were on him. Georgette put the basket down. She came close and ran her hand up the back of his neck beneath his hair. Magritte felt her fingers. His scalp electrified.
"Look at you," she said. "Your work, your dream life. It's always you. But here's what I've realized. You suffer."

She wrapped her arms around his head and held it. He leaned in, rested.

After a while she said, "The quiche smells good, the ham. I'll go make a salad."

She carried the basket into the kitchen.

His mother had been a milliner. The hats she'd made were beautiful. She had disappeared for the last time on a March night.

XVIII.

Fifty years later, after Georgette and Magritte were gone, after his paintings began to sell for large sums and those who'd mocked him were hastening to reverse themselves, biographers would make much of his not talking about his mother. But Magritte talked. Sometimes in bed at night he spoke frangible bits into the top of Georgette's head. He didn't have a final memory, just the swiftness of his mother's leaving and the cold, and nothing after that.

XIX.

Magritte had saved many of the hats his mother made. He ached with joy and terror when Georgette wore any one of them.

For Lucie in Dr. Scholl's Sandals

by David Blair

Maybe Lucie never went back home
much because there was less
Pittsburgh left, let it go
all at once rather than suffer
the many pieces
not in her books
of going, three movie theaters
gone, the one big screen
in the last one divvied
into five Green Stamps, the lawn
of the high school she hated
blown out, the Doric columns
obscured by the crown
of the new gym,
the old delicatessens
replaced by new ones,
the used books
and used records
and new books
and new records
vanished, the pieces
to the *Torah Chutes and Ladders*
vanished, the ice skating
rink of St. Edmund's Academy
gone, the J.C.C.
remodeled, with a clock tower,
Big Benjamin, Big Ben Yehuda

then obscured by the building
that went up where one
of three corner gas stations
became medical offices
and retail spaces,
the street cars
that rattled by her childhood,
in the sixties stopped,
and finally the worn penny-smooth
trolley tracks ripped out
and replaced by less bumpy
roadbed for busses
that pirated street car numbers
and vague hopes
of a bus-way connector
changes to the inner eye,
changes to the inner nose.
I could have looked up
and thought, *Hey weird*
pretty teenager,
go where I go
with great big hair
buying cigarettes
while I buy Milk Duds,
I am but five, but in love
with ladies my sister's age
because I look up to them
swinging on knee-length
braids down practically
to red Dr. Scholl's sandals,
but never did, as far
as I know, but possibly so,

from the pharmacy lady
harrumphing in her octagonal
pink glasses and red, white
and blue striped
pharmacy cashier coats
calmly advancing
through Gerald Ford,
and the old blind guy
sold unsharpened pencils
from a cup from the bank steps,
and a constellation
of nickels and dimes
across the afternoon paper
with the third inning scores
at the newsstand managed
by a clean-cut man
with a turtleneck, a corduroy
blazer and a tall afro,
and small change
into the fireman's boot
spangled with small red helmets.
St. Lucy, St. Francis, St. Christopher,
St. John the Evangelist, St. Gertrude,
St. Earth, the weird
painted postcard look
settles in with mist
and green light
in the forest primeval
of the Appalachian
public park named
for one major skinflint
or rich crook or another,

so I will keep things
light and misty as possible
rather than squatting
in the sulfur of the river
deeper than I can think
with night barges bending
foreshortening spotlights
gone walking in dank fog.
I maybe get saved awhile
in the noosphere
with other people
and a run of good luck
that won't matter at all
and the paper towels
and the flies
and the cheese
and the grapes
in the home kitchen
to keep things going
in the great indoor art
of knowing strangers.

Chapter Five: [How to Survive Deadly Diseases]

by Carrie Bennett

The following is a list of possible illnesses one may face during an expedition and the essential tools to survive.

LOST-FOG

> *Fire-mirrors,*
> *blanket shelter,*
stone saw,
> *opticompass, a pocket*
> *of seeds.*

GROUNDTHIRST

Hybranch,
> *hollowed-out*
> *drying cards,*
heavy matchsticks,
> *collapsible alarms,*
> *doorbags.*

BONEHUNGER

Flingknives, necknives, rubbleknives.

BURIED-THROAT DISEASE

>   *Furrowed tentscreen, a*
>   *fallowed nest.*
>   *lightstrip filters,*
> *radiocans.*

WOLF-ENVY

Alert-vaults, battle anxels,
>   *hatchet chain*
hitchsafe
>   *flashlight lightening*
>   *roadlamp.*

BIRCH SADNESS

>   *Throwing-set*
>   *feathers,*
>   *bruised doorburden,*
> *lightweight*
> *chest bundle,*
>   *a small trapdoor.*

Hiking Boots

by Rebecca Watkins

You were the Whore and the Beast of Babylon,
I was Rin Tin Tin.
— Leonard Cohen

During the summer of 2012, my brother, Seth, and my father began what would become an Appalachian Trail section hike tradition. They would pack their backpacks and trekking poles into my father's Prius and drive from Indianapolis, Indiana to Vermont, or Pennsylvania or West Virginia, or whatever state they had not yet walked. The section hikes were not done in order, north to south or south to north, but their goal was to use their summer vacations to hike the entire trail over the next ten years. It seemed that this was their time to bond as father and son; to feel like ragged men, tough and wild; to connect with nature; to voluntarily eat freeze-dried food; to be uncomfortable in the company of many trees; but mostly — to stare at the ground and at their shoes, while thinking about their swollen feet.

I was not part of this tradition.

I laughed when they came home, hardly able to walk, and asked why they would submit themselves to such misery. They told me I didn't understand. And I didn't. So they never invited me.

To my surprise and everyone else's, I invited myself in 2017 when I was twenty-four, after a breakup with my boyfriend of four years, whom I'll call Leo. I was in desperate need of some soul-searching. The pain was appealing to me. Maybe body pain would erase or at least numb my heart pain. I figured I wanted to reinvent myself — to become a person who took long hikes, owned trekking poles, and wore her hair in French braids and a bandana. Yes, this was the person I thought I should become.

Like Lorelai Gilmore in the Netflix reboot of *Gilmore Girls*, like Cheryl Strayed in *Wild*, like any woman who has lost herself, I needed something to change. More importantly, I needed time with myself, and away from the Indianapolis apartment I used to share with my ex.

At nineteen I planned on being married by twenty-five. It was part of my midwestern playbook. Living in Indianapolis and going to school in the suburbs, north of downtown, I had been conditioned, not through any direct teachings, but by observation and subtle comments here and there, to believe that marriage was a stepping stone, a rite of passage — just like getting my ears pierced at nine or being baptized at ten. It felt that it was important whether I was dating and how serious my relationships were. It wasn't uncommon for my friends to get married right after high school, or immediately following college. I came to believe it was essential to my becoming, and to my happiness. My sister, Rachael, had been married at twenty-five, and my parents even younger. At Rachael's wedding, people met Leo and told me I was next. It almost felt like a warning.

The idea of marriage, of a soulmate, of spending the rest of my life with someone other than myself had been implanted in my subconscious and woven into my life plan.

I didn't question it until my heart had been broken. The plan unraveled.

***

After several weeks of talking to friends and my family about the possibility of my joining the summer hike, I had completely talked myself into it. I would be hiking an average of about eight miles a day, on a mountain, for five days, while carrying thirty pounds on my back. I wasn't met with as much shock as I'd assumed I would, so I figured if they thought I could do it, I probably could.

I spent around $1300 on my gear which included a new backpack, a lightweight sleeping bag and a blow-up air mat, a water filter, freeze-dried food, electrolyte tablets, hiking pants, a head lamp, trekking poles, and a poop shovel.

I realized that it was only once I bought the gear that the same people who told me I should go began to take it seriously. My dad started meticulously planning our location, mileage and even booked the hotel rooms: one for the two of them, one for me. I was locked in. There was no turning back now.

My dad decided on the Virginia Triple Crown, which includes three well-known vistas: Dragon's Tooth, McAfee Knob and Tinker Cliffs. The Triple Crown totals 35 miles, and we were going to complete it within five days. The most popular of the vistas is McAfee Knob, a cliff on Catawba mountain in Virginia, and a prime AT destination — perhaps due in part to Bill Bryson's bestseller, *A Walk in The Woods*, and the Robert Redford film that followed. The McAfee Knob hike begins at 1,740' (530 m) and rises to a height of 3,197' (974 m) above sea level. It is approximately 4.4 miles to the top and takes from four to six hours. The parking lot is usually packed full of SUVs, Hybrids with bike racks, and Jeeps. The Knob has become so popular, it may be close to impossible to experience the 270° view in solitude.

***

Before I set off on this grand adventure, I trained. I went with my dad to the gym almost every day with a backpack I filled with play sand from our garage. I power-walked on a treadmill, incline seven, to work on the steeps. I took on the Stairmaster but never mastered it. I even lifted weights. All of this was fueled by my rebound boyfriend, whom I'll call Jessie, who is ten years my senior and a man of many identities: math professor, motorcyclist, housebuilder, HGTV acolyte, and motto collector. One such motto was: *deadlift and squat, body gonna pop.*

After having briefly mentioned the possibility that I might get off the trail if it proved too difficult, or my father and brother went too fast, Jessie offered me this warning: "If you get off the trail, I won't be able to date you." He claimed to be joking later, but it always seems that jokes reveal some truth.

About twice a week I would meet Jessie at Marian University where he taught advanced mathematics, and we would walk from his office to the gym and spend an hour lifting. He became my trainer. He admitted that he did it because of the view of my ass. He was always a little too honest.

During these months of training, I learned that my white-washed high-tops made better lifting shoes than my running sneakers. I learned that I needed to roll the deadlift bar up my legs and under no circumstances arch my back. I learned that I shouldn't fear the squat bar tumbling on top of me as long as I had my safety bars at the right height and balanced the bar below my neck, but above my shoulders. I learned that I could learn these things. I learned that I could be strong.

I also learned that once Jessie noticed my butt getting stronger and less squishy, he stopped inviting me to his university gym. *Eww, it is getting hard. Don't lose the jiggle.*

Men have always been vocal about their preferences for my appearance. I can first remember really noticing it in my junior year of high school when the first real boyfriend I ever had asked me how much I weighed right after I had demolished a burrito at the Chipotle across from our high school. Up until this point in my life, I'd felt perfectly comfortable with my weight and height, 5'4".

125, I told him.

He scanned me up and down, *Okay, well don't go past 130...oh and stop biting your nails. That's not an attractive habit.*

From then on, it continued with each consecutive boyfriend, and eventually I just accepted that I needed to look a certain way in order to be loved, or desired. I wore my hair straight when they liked it that way. I wore heels. I wore a lot of makeup for one boyfriend, and none for another who thought natural was best. I made myself up to meet the expectations of the guys I dated.

While training for the trail I found that I could distract myself from the sharp abdominal cramps I felt while running and the burning of my lungs by thinking about this trip with Leo and remembering how he, and so many others, made me question my own worth because of my weight, or my wavy undyed hair that curls a little too much on the inside, or my off-again-on-again acne, or my nail biting habits — all of the things they saw and didn't like. These thoughts fueled my workouts and I felt, more than any pain, the immeasurable desire for revenge. My revenge would be to prove that I could climb a mountain, that I had determination and strength. I needed to prove to myself that I could do hard things, but mostly I felt I had to prove to my ex that I could do hard things. I wanted to make him regret breaking up with me — to feel like he'd made a mistake and that I was, in fact, the adventurous, in-shape, outdoorsy girl who wears cargo shorts with hiking boots to the farmer's market even though she isn't a farmer or someone who shops at Eddie Bauer.

I wanted to transfer my pain to him through means of one picture I planned to take atop McAfee's ledge and then post to Facebook. I imagined that would do the trick.

As I huffed and puffed on the incline treadmill I was transported back to a hot day in Utah. Summer of 2015, one year before the breakup, Leo and I decided to take a trip to explore various cities and think about where our forever home might be. On our way to California, we drove through Utah and decided we had some extra time to stop and take a hike in the Arches National Park. It was mid-afternoon and hot — so hot that I imagined we could pop out some cookie dough and bake cookies on the dashboard.

We found the trailhead to Delicate Arch and stepped out into the desert. He didn't think we needed water. He said that there was no need to carry it with us.

We walked over to where the trail began. The sign read, *Moderate Difficulty.* "See," he said. "Not hard. Let's go."

***

At first, I believed Leo when he said I would be fine without water. The terrain was rather flat, and I found that we could stop occasionally for fun pictures of us peeking out from rock windows. It seemed like it would continue to be a simple jaunt to a giant rock arch.

And then I saw it — the slab of a rock floor that tiled skyward, as if welcoming us to heaven — a sign I was being summoned to my death.

With the incline came labored breathing. I tried to hide my heaving and muffle the sound, only making it worse. I played with my hair and focused my gaze on the ground. With a strong tendency to trip, fall, tumble, twist, crash, and topple, I had to be careful with each step placement.

Gradually, the rocks grew in size and number. My steps took even longer
to plan, and I had to slow down as the hill steepened. My tortured breaths
became obvious and my throat began to burn. Leo was already twenty feet
in front of me and occasionally looked back to make sure I was still there.

"I think I need to stop for a second."

"Really?" he asked, "We're almost there."

I decided that my best plan of action was to blame my exhaustion on the
lack of water, which had more than likely been at least part of my problem.
He didn't buy it and tried to leave me behind so that I could just go at my
own pace and he wouldn't get bored waiting for me.

When I made it to the arch, we took some pictures, but I could tell he was
embarrassed by my struggle through the hike.

We got back to the car after dark and decided to find food in the town
nearby. We parked and walked to the first restaurant we saw. During
dinner we brainstormed our next day's activities and driving route and then
he asked. "So, that was really hard for you, huh?"

I said, "I guess but it would have been easier with water."

We got into the car and began the drive to our Airbnb. We rolled down
the windows, opened the sunroof and blasted Enya. The wind was cool and
sticky.

After the song was over and the silence between us crept again to the
foreground, he said softly, looking ahead at the road, "Maybe you should

start trying to lose weight."

When I didn't say anything, he continued, "Look, I don't want to be mean, but I'm not really attracted to you right now. I think you need to lose like thirty pounds." He looked over at me. I could see his gaze from the corner of my eye. He placed his hand gently on my thigh. "Lose thirty pounds by next year, or we may need to break up." At that moment, a sensation rose within me to open the car door and jump.

**

Some say that a woman can be seen along the edge of McAfee Knob, staring down into the foliage beneath the cliff, beckoning to an unwitting hiker to fall. When we camped after our hike to Dragon's Tooth we were joined by a group of through-hikers — the hikers who brave the entire 2,200-mile trail all in one go. They told us the story of a young woman from the 1700s with auburn hair and a dress and cape of red. The story goes that she leapt off McAfee Knob from a broken heart. It is said that her ghost comes back to the mountain each year on July 23rd, presumably the day she jumped to her death, searching for men she can lure into jumping off with her. If they refuse or resist, she'll push them off and follow them down.

"Don't let her get'cha," the hikers teased Seth. It was July 21st. Our plan was to get to the top of McAfee on July 23rd — right on time to see the ghost of the Scarlet Woman.

After what seemed like a full day of hiking, we reached the McAfee Knob trailhead. Seth sprinted ahead. "You're too slow for me," he taunted. Seth, like my father, is a dedicated distance runner. I don't know how I missed this gene.

There were other groups on the trail that day, some through-hikers, some families who'd driven their cars to the trailhead, and Seth was determined to stay ahead of all of them. My dad stayed behind with me, coaching me up the mountain. "Just lean in, Beks. Look at the ground and walk."

I had trained hard for this. I was in better shape than I'd ever been. Even in high school gym I couldn't run a mile without counting stars by the end.

I broke into a cold sweat and told my dad I needed to find a sitting rock. I got out my trail mix and filtered water and focused on controlling my breath. My mom had insisted that we each bring electrolyte tablets for our water, and as usual, it was a good suggestion. I felt a little better after a few minutes and my father, anxious to get to the famous knob, urged me to buck up and start moving. I gritted my teeth, hauled my heavy backpack over my shoulders, plugged in my playlist and started upward over the mountain, Iron & Wine in my ears.

Music distracted me for a while, but all I wanted to do was cry. I hadn't pooped for days, I was bloated, my knees were popping, and my shoulders were forming noticeable strap burns. I broke one of my trekking poles the first day between two rocks climbing up Dragon's Tooth, and my feet had already blistered.

I looked at the happy families around me, enjoying their day hike — nothing but water in their hands and car keys in their pockets.

A young girl, maybe four, skipped up the mountain with a Barbie in one hand and a lollipop in the other. I wished I was that young girl and could put my hands up in the air and demand to be held or hop along finding magic in the smallest of places without the weight on my back which ultimately seemed to weigh less than the weight of male expectations I carried. Was I really doing this for me, or for these men who told me how

I should shape myself and made me feel like I had to prove my worth? I had become a mold to them. Something that could be chipped away at, shaped, manipulated, improved.

***

A few months after Leo and I broke up, I was dating Jessie — the math professor, who decided, after he heard my plan to hike a section of the Appalachian Trail, that he wanted not only to help me weight train for the hike, but also to buy my hiking boots. His sister came with us to R.E.I. and whispered: "You know he is buying these so when you look at the ground, you'll think of him." He heard her say this and winked at me.

I couldn't help but smile.

We browsed the boots and found two pairs that I really liked.

"Let's get you the cute ones," he told me.

"But they don't have as much arch or ankle support," I countered. "I think I need to get the other pair because I have flat feet."

My boot choice was green and blue; he liked the pink and maroon — more fitting for his Pretty Young Thing, as he called me.

When I made my choice, he scrunched his face and slowly worked himself into a nod, "Okay, if that's what you really want. But just know that people on my team don't have flat feet." He shook his finger at me, did a little dance, and directed me to the socks.

I let him buy the hiking boots, two pairs of wool socks, and arched inserts. His sister was right; I did end up thinking a lot about him while struggling up the mountain.

 I thought about how much I believed that if I got off the trail and failed to walk the full 35 miles of The Triple Crown, he wouldn't want me anymore. I thought about how much that scared me.

***

When my dad and I made it to the top of McAfee Knob, we found Seth dangling his legs from the cliff. "Woah, be careful there," I teased. "You don't want to fall off — or be pushed."

"Ha, I don't think I'm the one we have to worry about falling," he countered. I winked and then stuck out my tongue at him because I knew he was right. I am the clumsy one.

I did a quick scan around the Knob, paying close attention to the trees behind us.

I was looking for the Scarlet Woman.

I knew I wouldn't be able to see her, even as I pushed my mind to begin believing in ghosts, because the legend says she appears only to men. But I still looked, despite this. I hoped that perhaps she'd appear to me because we felt some similar pain and she'd beckon me to join her in her revenge.

I stood near the edge of the cliff and looked out into the scene before me. There was significant foliage right beneath the cliff, and it almost looked like a fall would be softened by the bushes below. I raised my hands into the air like a bird preparing to take flight as a gust of wind propelled me forward. I was far enough from the edge of the cliff that my step forward was caught, and I regained my balance. Shaken, I moved backwards, and turned to walk from the cliff to where Seth and my dad sat, feasting on jerky and dried banana chips.

As we sat there on the rock, I remembered my own urge to jump, not off a cliff, but out of a car, and out of that life. I imagined the Scarlet Woman sitting on the edge, peering down into the pit of trees below, trying to assuage her sorrow. Did she really want to die, or just escape for a while and take temporary leave from the pain?

***

After completing our hike, I researched the Scarlet Woman, hoping to find something in her story to redeem the actions of her ghostly counterpart. I found almost nothing but links to biblical stories of Babylon. Of course, the name, Scarlet Woman, is not unique. The woman most known as the Scarlet Woman, or the Scarlet Beast, has no connection to the Appalachian Trail.

The only actual evidence that the story we heard wasn't made up on the spot can be found in a blog called Alchetron, which borrows facts about the Knob and its history from Wikipedia — with the exception of one section called Folklore/ Legends, which reads:

The Scarlet Woman — It has been believed that on the 23rd of July, a very pretty woman with red hair, wearing an old-fashioned red dress sometimes appears on the Knob. She is usually seen only by men and is said to be the spirit of a woman who had jumped to her death at the site on July 23 over a century ago. As the legend goes, the Scarlet Woman beckons men to join her in jumping off the edge and will sometimes attempt to push them off.

Although this is not what I would consider a totally credible source, it was the only trace of the story I could find outside of the trail. This internet account says she jumped, which matches the story we were told on the trail, but it doesn't give any kind of backstory or motive for her falling to her death. One may conclude that her death was related to heartbreak as her revenge is targeted at men. Although hikers may occasionally get oral tidbits of her tale, her true story may never be pieced together.

I tried to imagine her story and to understand what might have caused her not only to jump, but to be compelled in the afterlife to haunt the cliff and the men who get too close to the edge.

***

As I lay in my tent that night of our Knob hike, I worked to drive my pain to the surface — to identify its source. I felt the muscles in my shoulders, sore from backpack straps; I felt my knees, heavy from carrying me for miles; I felt my feet, blistered and wet; I felt my lower back, aching from bending over on the steeps; I felt my body, alive and pulsing. Still, I couldn't excavate the pain buried deep within my heart.

Nearing sleep, I imagined the Scarlet Woman's heartbreak. I tried to piece her story together, but it kept conflating with my own, until her pain was my pain, and mine hers. But how could I really know her pain or compare it to mine?

I didn't jump.

I stayed in the car and stayed with these men. I allowed them to mold me until they ran out of clay.

As a child I made up ghost stories — stories I didn't believe and had no reason to believe. Ghosts are notorious for having unresolved pain, tasks or things left unsaid. The Scarlet Woman seems to seek revenge, remains bitter, unforgiving, and perhaps there is something about her story that may redeem this, but mine would not. I took her with me as a reminder that I must determine my own fate — that I can breathe through the pain, even on an incline with weight on my back, and that with each step, the weight seems to lighten a little.

I completed the hike and took the picture atop McAfee Knob and posted it to Facebook, but by then I had unfriended my ex. When I saw Jessie, he congratulated me on my completion of the hike and I made a point not to tell him that at the end of the hike, when my father and my brother determined they wanted to go a bit further, I determined I'd stay back, get myself a fried chicken dinner, pop into Goodwill for some retail therapy, and settle into a hotel, freshly showered, feet throbbing, but happier and more satisfied than I'd never felt.

Did You See an Asian Man Hiking in the Woods?

by Allen Gee

While we had been in the Adirondack Mountains at Tupper Lake since early June, it wasn't until mid-July when I could finally hike alone. My wife encouraged me, so now at 1:30pm I felt nervous and excited — like the runner I used to be at the starting line before a distance race. I'd stuffed a knapsack with two water bottles, a hunk of aged cheddar cheese, and several Ritz crackers. For fishing, I'd added a small bag with hooks, split shot, and Panther Martin spinners. I'd decided to bring a five-and-a-half foot graphite rod with a reliable, old Garcia Mitchell 308 spinning reel. The forecast called for a 77% chance of thunderstorms, but on many days when rain was predicted, it simply hadn't fallen. Still, out of caution I crammed a raincoat and rain pants into a compartment. Wearing hiking shorts, a t-shirt, a plaid shirt, and good hiking boots, I realized this was my first opportunity in over forty years to hike by myself in the mountains. At fifty-eight years old, I hoped I was up to the challenge.

Although I'd once run long distances, after a heart operation eight years before, I'd lessened any serious training, and sometimes, it seemed, my overall ambition. But by 2:30pm I parked at the gate for the Bog River Trail, my truck the sole vehicle. The brown and yellow trail sign read: Goodman Bridge 0.2 miles; Round Lake Outlet 1.8 miles; Winding Falls 2.8 miles; State Route 421-West Trailhead 5.3 miles. After texting a photo of the sign to my wife, I set off.

My plan was to try fishing and walking the 2.8 miles to Winding Falls, then retrace my steps, hoping that my endurance would be sufficient.

It only took a few minutes to cover the .2 miles to Goodman Bridge. Goodman Mountain had been named for Andrew Goodman, who had been a summer resident of Tupper Lake, but had been killed by Klansmen in Mississippi during the 1964 Freedom Summer for attempting to advocate for Black voting rights. The bridge was named for Andrew's father.

The naming of the bridge and mountain intrigued me, but also reminded me of the racial difference in predominantly white Tupper Lake. I hadn't seen other Asian hikers during three previous hiking trips up mountains with my daughter that June, so I didn't anticipate seeing another Asian on the Bog River Trail. After crossing the Goodman Bridge, I sidestepped down to the wide and slow-moving Bog River. No fish darted out to strike the yellow Panther Martin spinner I cast out, and after a few minutes I moved on, the trail angling southwest like a well-worn passage between the Bog River to the east and an unnamed 1,800-foot mountain to the west. I forded small creeks where rocks and logs had been set down to make crossings easier. Thick mud covered the ground since rainfall had saturated everything. *I have to be careful,* I thought. *I can't slip or fall, especially hiking alone.*

As the trail skirted fern beds, my worries multiplied and my mind conjured bears. Two days before, my daughter and I had seen one lumber across the road in front of us with all of the immensity of a bulldozer — not far off on Rt. 421 on our way to swim at Horseshoe Lake. I had no bear spray, knife, or firearm now, so if I encountered a bear, my life could easily be over.

I thought again of being the sole Asian on the trail — if I somehow ran into other hikers, I'd certainly by the only Asian. Since early June, the only other Asians I'd seen in Tupper Lake were the family that owned and worked at the China Wok in town. A real estate agent had recently told me about how a local property owner whose house — covered with anti-Democratic signs and the Confederate flag — offended many people, but the owner couldn't be forced to remove anything because of freedom of speech. Racism was obviously present in the far north; I had concerns about it, as do so many minorities in America, regardless of where they are. The fear mongering by Trump calling Covid-19 the "China virus" and the subsequent rise of assaults against elderly Asian Americans in New York and California, along with the the shootings of Asian women in Atlanta, also preyed upon my thoughts.

Fear didn't dominate my entire being, though. No, part of the point of hiking for me was to try and leave all that behind, to truly escape the confines of race for a little while, and so I physically and psychologically kept moving on. I focused on how my feet, ankles, calves, knees, lower back, and shoulders felt. Over the years, aside from heart surgery, I'd had bone spurs removed and a torn labrum repaired in my right shoulder. My back had seized up and hampered me a few times walking before. And if my heart beat rapidly, I feared being in atrial fibrillation. Fortunately, for now, everything felt fluid and smooth, like my heart was a dependable engine in a reliable car.

Deer flies and horse flies buzzed my head like miniature drones, so I put on a baseball cap and logged at least a mile. As well-marked as the trail was, I still hoped that I was on the right trail and then felt grateful hearing the Bog River again. The trail descended and soon paralleled the Bog. I felt excited about fishing, but the river looked too shallow, the water tea-colored, tinged brown from decomposing organic matter. This was usually a sign of healthy water in the Adirondacks, but I'd been told the fishing in the Bog wasn't very good. I still hoped to catch a trout or two, maybe even one to keep for dinner. If needed, I'd hike with the perseverance of a backcountry guide through the worst brush or bramble to reach a likely spot.

I heard faster moving water and then spotted a long, deep pool at least ten yards across with submerged rocks and a fast sluice of current spilling out. Since a fish could be lying in wait, my spirits rose. I stepped quietly onto rocks at the head of the pool, cast the Panther Martin spinner, and caught a small yellow perch. I sighed since perch weren't what I was after. After several more casts, nothing else struck the lure, so the eerie possibility settled in my mind that due to the pool's being right by the trail, the water was fished over already, any trout long since gone.

After several hundred more yards, a second pool presented itself right by the trail. When I cast, nothing pursued the spinner, so I hastened away, the trail veering from the riverbank to higher, more open ground. In time, I spotted a slow moving pool below that I could only reach by bushwhacking through high weeds and blown down trees. The pool looked good, filled with logs and rocks, so I pushed aside branches, climbed over tree trunks, and stepped carefully, making my way down.

As I cast by the shadowy depths near a large rock, a fish rose and swiped at my Panther Martin spinner. In that instant, I recognized the hooked jaw and bright-colored spots of a native brook trout. Suddenly the fish freed itself from the hook as if it'd decided it didn't want to be caught by a mere mortal like myself. Humbled, I thought *At least I'd seen a trout in the Bog River.*

Deer flies and horse flies pestered the top of my head and the back of my neck as I started off again, retracing my steps through the blow downs. Eventually, the trail descended and stayed along the river, and after a time, I discovered a long deep pool fed by rushing water. My eyes read the current like a guide would have, gauging that the deeper stretch in the middle might hold a fish. Stepping carefully, I hopped from rock to rock until reaching a cluster of large boulders. As relief swept through me that I'd made it without falling, I sat on the flattest rock above the water.

After I caught my breath and relaxed, the river rushing around me on all sides further soothed my mind. Due to the air currents stemming from the river's passage, a constant wind filled the air around me, preventing any bugs from landing. Time seemed to slow; I felt a sense of peacefulness that I hadn't felt during the entire past thirteen months since the Covid-19 pandemic had begun.

I smiled. Along with the sense of being enveloped by nature, I felt content. *Somehow I need to retire early,* I thought and could have sat there for an eternity.

After drinking half a bottle of water, I cast the Panther Martin into the run by the shore and let the spinner tumble with the current. Nothing bit, but then I cast directly downstream in front of me and retrieved the spinner through where the fast water flattened out. I felt the bump of a fish taking the lure, and the graphite rod bent sharply.

I saw the silver blur of a trout leaping out of the water. The fish splashed back down, zipped towards the river's eastern bank, and the line tightened. I kept reeling and finally brought the trout to my feet, keeping it in the water. It was an eight-inch brook trout; I marveled at the silver, purple, red and yellow palette of its colors and carefully reached down and worked the hook from its mouth. As the fish swam off, I gazed around and felt giddy, marking the spot, hoping it would stay in my memory.

I felt satisfied and happy and sat absorbing the tranquility of the river's splashes and watching the leaves being moved by soft breezes. The river, I thought, would remain there as long as it was left unharmed. I slowly worked my way back across the rocks to the shore, and, hiking again, I decided not to stop until I reached Winding Falls.

The trail broke away from the river and led up and down hills and through more broad fern glades, between white birch stands, and through majestic forests of balsam firs. After more than two miles, the trail returned to the river, which was now slower and wider now, obstructed in places by beaver dams.

Grasses rubbed against my shins above my hiking socks as I negotiated overgrown trail sections. I hoped there wasn't poison ivy. The river narrowed and soon my ears discerned the roaring sound of tumbling water — it had to be the waterfall.

I spotted the falls to the south. The trail curved around the falls, though, and I wanted to see them up close. I reached a sign that read it was 2.8 miles back to Goodman Bridge and State Route 421, and 2.5 miles on the Winding Falls Trail to the State Route 421 West Trailhead. Checking the time, I saw that it was 5:30pm, and realized there was no cell phone signal. I told myself to be mindful because darkness fell at around 8:00 pm. The rarity struck me of how I still hadn't seen another human being; part of me felt safe due to the solitude, but it'd taken three hours to reach the falls. Still wanting to see them up close, I backtracked and found a worn side path.

The spur cut closer to the Bog River directly above the falls where the water churned, and soon I stared from a rocky crag overlooking the falls at tons of water cascading eight feet down. My ears heard only the din of the endless torrent. Caution pinged inside me; careful to not stand too close to the crag's edge, I felt insignificant, there for only a short time on the planet while the falls had been plunging sharply downward for a millennium.

To my left, I noticed two smooth memorial stones. One read, *Dad There is Never Enough Time,* the other, *PA Memories Never To Be Forgotten.* Both markers were for a man named Hebe Costello who had leased a cabin nearby until he passed away. It felt easy to intuit how someone would want to be buried there, perhaps with ashes interred or scattered in the currents, or how the family had wanted to leave the memorial stones there for perpetuity. I'd later see in writings about the falls, and on maps, how some called the spot Pa's Falls. The stones made the overlook feel solemn and more cherished, like a sacred space. The falls beyond the gravesite poured down sharply to the southeast in a level trough, and then came a second vertical drop, the falls spilling on an eastern course down a large granite hill. Returning to the side path, I descended to the base of the falls where I cast the Panther Martin spinner but had no strikes. Fishing didn't matter so much; the sun was lowering at what seemed like a faster rate. My phone revealed it was 6:00pm. *Why is there never enough time for so many of us in the wilderness?* I thought. *Our journeys are always too brief. While the Greenland Shark or the Giant Tortoise can live for hundreds of years, we're on limited time.*

I tugged the rain pants out of my knapsack and pulled them over my shorts so I could hike without worrying about walking through the overgrown sections of the trail. I regretted not having better more breathable hiking pants. Common sense told me to rehydrate; I finished the first bottle of water.

I figured it would be best to hike straight out. My wife would be concerned despite how I'd told her I might not be back until dark. Setting out with a full stride, and since the air still held the heat of the day, I quickly grew warmer, perspiring more.

As much as I wanted to hike non-stop, after half a mile, rounding a bend along the river, I halted, sensing eyes were upon me. Then I saw a beaver was watching me, its head and back floating above the surface. We stared at each other. I remembered hearing how beavers could actually become aggressive. Once when I was fishing at Lake George, a beaver had slapped its tail repeatedly as I steered my boat too close to its thatched den on the eastern shoreline. I'd also heard that beavers preferred not to be seen and would always submerge to seek cover. But as I brought out my cell phone to take a photo, the beaver remained motionless in front of me, not seeing me as a threat, but as an object of curiosity. We kept staring at each other, as if we each knew no harm existed between us. I stood outside of time, caught up, appreciatively sharing the woods with this other animal. When the beaver finally swam away, I videotaped it for a long while since it moved slowly, staying above the surface. Did I know how lucky I was to see such a creature behaving without fear? I knew. Then I started walking once more, my concern about the sun going down returning; maybe I'd lingered too long. I thought I could hike a mile in half an hour, though, which would put me back at the trailhead around 7:30pm.

My legs and shoulders felt sore. Fatigue, after such a strenuous afternoon, was catching up with me. The rain pants, although keeping my shins from being irritated by grasses and brambles, were retaining warmth.

I kept on, but several uphill stretches significantly winded me. My heart, I realized, was beating fast. Since my breaths were more labored, I felt older, suddenly more vulnerable. I pressed on, not wanting to falter, but with each passing step my feet felt heavy, not as easy to pick up, and upon cresting a long hill, I attempted to hike with a fuller stride, but my legs refused. Lactic acid, I thought, had accumulated, weakening my calves and hamstring muscles. The long hill had significantly diminished me, and then on a short flat stretch that should have been easy to traverse, my left foot didn't step high enough and caught on a tree root.

Damn. I fell hands and face first, at least, but with a full body sprawl. Picking myself up, I sat and felt stunned but took inventory. My hands were scraped, but I hadn't injured a knee or ankle — no broken bones hindered me, as well — yet at the same time, I thought that if I'd hurt myself badly in any other way, I was nearly two miles from the trailhead. *Was I too old to hike alone? If I became hurt, out of cell phone range, how long would it be until my wife summoned DEC rangers, and the call would go out, Did you see an Asian man hiking in the woods?*

I opened the second water bottle and drank half of it. I stood, started walking again, and felt glad that I seemed to be all right. As I passed through parts of the forest with thicker balsam firs, the light was dimmed so sunset felt more imminent. My heart rate was still fast, my breaths strained. *Keep going,* I thought. But at least I was going.

The trail paralleled the Bog River for a while. At a slow section, I stopped and ate some of the cheese and crackers that were in my knapsack. *What a strange thing,* I thought, *to be eating sharp cheddar aged 7 years and to be simultaneously battling exhaustion.*

I covered more ground and took out my phone and saw a text from my wife; somewhere, I'd gotten back into range. *Are you alright?* she was asking. I texted back that I was fine and on my way out. She texted back, *Okay.*

Was I fine?

The trail swung northeast away from the river. After walking for a long while, I realized my breathing had settled down, and I was maintaining a steady pace, as if I'd picked up a second wind after four a half miles of hiking. I'd been smart to rehydrate and eat a little. As tired as I felt, I thought, *This isn't so bad.*

I still hadn't seen anyone else. The woods remained like another country, and I realized not a drop of rain had fallen all afternoon; the weather reports had been wrong again. Since the river wasn't audible, and even with trail markers in sight, I hoped once more that I was heading in the right direction, as if I could have somehow turned onto the Round Lake Outlet Trail. I felt like any kind of mistake having gone so far would put me at a great risk. But then I noticed a birch tree that had fallen to the side of the trail, and perceiving that it looked familiar, I knew I was okay. Deer flies still dive-bombed around my head; I swatted one from my neck, and then reaching where a small stream cut through the muddy trail, I stepped carefully across on wet rocks, trying to avoid soaking my boots.

As I returned through more fern groves, along the side of the unnamed 1,800-foot mountain, I questioned once more what I'd do if a bear — or worse yet a bear with cubs — interrupted my private quest, this solo expedition playing out on a post middle-age scale. Would I equip myself with bear spray next time? I'd hiked for years as a teenager in the Adirondacks before moving away without thinking about needing any kind of bear deterrent, but since then people had encroached too much on the forests, leaving wild animals with not enough land of their own. My supposedly more progressive older generation hadn't treated the planet any better than past generations. And we'd been worse, with global warming and its onslaught of hurricanes and droughts and wildfires now occurring regularly across the country, so I thought I needed to become even more vocal in my support for reforms.

Now since my heart rate had slowed, and considering my age, I judged that I was fine. No chest pains of any sort slowed or deterred me. My wind was still manageable. I could certainly still hike alone. I kept walking, and for a long while, I felt the pleasurable sensation of moving across the earth under my own power, like any other creature out in the wild. I felt grateful that I could still be like a deer or antelope, or become calmer in the middle of the river, or commune with a beaver in another kind of quiet. Sweat soaked my t-shirt and shorts and the lining of the long rain pants, but the last leg of the hike was all that remained.

I still have some solo hiking left in me, I thought with a measure of satisfaction. I felt glad that my wife hadn't needed to send out any kind of alert. I remembered now that I'd fallen before while hiking when I was much younger, and I'd picked myself up then and felt fortunate to be uninjured. Who was to say that falling now should discourage me? *I might*, I thought, *need some hiking poles for stability in the near future, and that wouldn't be the worst thing.* What the mountains offered alone — the fishing, the solace, the time away — was still more than enough to outweigh any risks or perils.

And the Adirondacks still offered a respite for me from the outside world's pressing issues of race and culture; it was a relief knowing there was a place where I could peacefully hike and fish alone. I thought, however, of how I also wouldn't mind seeing more people of color in these same woods; I didn't need to be the only one. These days prospective hikers of color only needed to study maps or consult hiking books like I had to find out where to go, and of course there was the internet, with its web pages telling all. We didn't need to wait to be invited or made to feel welcome by anyone; no, I would have never hiked or fished anywhere if I'd waited for that. But for any first time hiker, I'd recommend going with someone.

When I reached the Goodman Bridge, it was 7:15pm. I figured I'd covered 2.8 miles in just over an hour, taking a little additional time to commune with the beaver and then pick myself up after falling. I shucked off the rain pants and saw fish of some sort were rising, feeding on insects on the Bog River's smooth surface maybe forty yards to the north. I made a mental note of the location, and after stuffing the rain pants back in my knapsack, drank the last of my water. The sun was getting low; stillness predominated the land. I took in the remaining blue of the sky and beheld the dense white clouds, and hearing frogs peeping everywhere, I wanted to hold such a feeling of being surrounded by only nature within me like a shield, or carry it as a reminder of how there are spaces without contention.

At the trailhead, my truck waited, undisturbed, on the other side of the gate. I still hadn't seen another person the entire time. Where else could I find this depth of solitude? There were many outdoor spaces, I knew, but since this region was where I'd grown up fishing I felt extremely fortunate that I could temporarily traverse it again. I vowed to return and hike more, hopefully a substantial number of miles, for as long as my mind and body would allow.

The Mighty Mississippi, August 29, 2021

by Pamela Wax

What alarmed you, O sea, that you fled?
River Jordan, that you ran backward?
— Psalms 114:5

After the thrill-flash in the storm-dark,
chant-count your prayers, a child's wish
for crash-boom: *One Mississippi, two*
Mississippi, three… rhythmic until the measured
truth cracks, redounding in glass panes,
floorboards, and our bones   the epiphany of an eye,
a storm, a blink of a mile or five, or one too distant
for danger.   Nature runs its course:
          The Gulf Stream is warm and swift,
          birds migrate, you age, loved ones die,
          matter cannot be created or destroyed,
          the Ol' Man flows south to the delta
until it doesn't.   Until Ida runs
its course into the ground,   and your dead
splash all around you, laughing.

Kingwood, West Virginia

by Dorothy Shubow Nelson

I almost died in West Virginia, not from the cold or heat—
in winter there are dead trees to burn, in summer the Cheat River.
Perhaps I would have died laughing or crying or dancing or
falling off a tractor while making a sharp turn up a hill.

I almost died of heartbreak for all the losses—cave-ins,
explosions, black lung, murders, mine wars, drugs, medical
malpractice or no practice at all, from bulldozers on mountains,
from unregulated logging, from inequity, or from heartbreak
leaving behind—road trips, the rally in Harlan, court battles,
the beer garden, picnics, mountains, woodlands,

      the people.

I bow my head to a gravestone, know how much it takes to save
a loved one's life, to stretch it out far beyond what the Docs thought
was possible—not to believe data, the diagnosis and prognosis,
not to leave the bedside
                  that your loved ones should live
no matter what—not to leave

      to stand tall and straight with life in your hands breathing
swearing that you could keep standing like that, life in both hands.

I wrap my arms around the gravestones, trees, remnants of history
    in view of these mountains
          formed 480 million years ago

                that dare us to tear them down.

Playing Chicken

by Scott Gould

I am a home health nurse for Williamsburg County. My present occupation has not caused me to be shot at, molested, or otherwise screwed with because I am six feet, four inches tall and weigh two hundred and sixty-five pounds and have an attitude that repels ridicule like the back side of a magnet. The last time someone attempted humor in regard to me being a male nurse, I broke his nose. Then, I set it for him. I am a nurse because it required very little money and effort to get into tech school classes when I took leave of Parris Island, a garden spot where I lost both of my big toenails and sixteen pounds while I learned to be a war machine.

That is all to say that between then and now, I have put many a mile on my Plymouth Valiant, negotiating the swampy two-ruts of this county where people have more concern for the lotto numbers than their health. I have calculated the blood pressure of people who exist two ticks from a heart attack. I have listened to the sloshing lungs of those who smell like the insides of an ashtray. And I have wedged medicine spoons between the brown teeth of children who squirm like eels on hot sand. Through it all, I have come to believe that the human body is nothing more than a private trash heap that some of us fill to capacity faster than others.

Yet I do not come to preach. I come today with a message, and it is this: Folks you wouldn't normally put together are winding up under the same roof. And they are getting along.

Not only are they getting along, they are growing intimately familiar and consequently having babies, crisscrossing boundaries like smugglers with a bag of dope and a bad sense of direction. It is perhaps a health situation to monitor.

Think about this:

Some months ago, I pulled the Valiant onto a road that paralleled a set of
railroad tracks. Behind me, the tracks ran toward a pair of hills, where they
disappeared into a curve of green trees growing so close to the tracks, the
limbs were shaved and bare on one side from the constant scrape of freight
cars. In front of me, the tracks eventually pulled up behind the Victoria
Chicken Plant, where the slogan is right there, in big letters across the front
of the building: *We Are Why The Chickens Cross The Road.*

During shift changes, groups of Hispanic men, wearing black hip boots
and long white coats, walk between the plant and any number of trailer
parks tucked in the trees along the tracks. I have an EMT buddy who gets
summoned to the chicken plant once or twice a month when a line worker
loses a finger to a bone saw or slips and hits his head and nearly drowns
in the chicken goop on the floor. He says walking into the chicken plant is
like strolling straight through the gates of hell. He told me once there isn't
enough money in the world to make him spend a shift in the chicken plant,
and I told him he hadn't been poor enough yet. I would work there before
I'd starve. I just wouldn't eat chicken tenders anymore. I would adapt.

I was searching for a trailer park called — swear to God — Camelot.
Number sixty-five. My patient notes said that a Chevy Nova would be
parked outside the trailer. I never saw an official Camelot sign, just rode
through little clusters of mud-stained trailers until I ultimately turned
into a gravel driveway and spotted the Nova. It was bright yellow with a
back end jacked up in the direction of ten o'clock. It appeared some sort
of unwashed animal had expired on the front dash, the clay-colored fur
matted against the window. Enough religious icons to save a small town
from holy terror dangled from the rearview mirror along with a silvery
CD. The car was running, leaking gray smoke, not from where the exhaust
pipe should be, but from a hole in the undercarriage. The engine noise

reminded me of some hearts I had heard through my stethoscope, those on the near side of complete breakdown. Somebody was warming up the car, getting ready to leave.

I knocked on the door and heard the growl rise from under the steps. I knew there would be a dog. There *always* has to be a dog. Dogs come as standard equipment on my patients' homes. Alarm systems on four legs. Cheap and mean and won't quit when the power goes out. I'm never unprepared. I simply bent and put my head close to the top step. And I growled back. In five years, there hasn't been a dog that returned my call of the wild.

I felt in my front pocket for the little card of health-related Spanish sayings. I used this cheat sheet to get through visits in the area around the chicken plant. With my little card, I could say things like "Where does it hurt?" and "When was the last time you went to the bathroom?" and "You'd better see a doctor before you drop dead of a heart attack." Most of the chicken plant people spoke more English than I could Spanish. We always worked out our communication problems one way or the other.

The door opened, and the way the sun hit the screen door, I couldn't see anything or anyone through the sudden glare. "*Hola*," I said to a thin silhouette that appeared in the open space.

"You from the department?" a woman asked back.

When I said yes, the screen door opened and I walked into the most amazing shrine to NASCAR I had ever seen in my life. In a single quick glance, I couldn't pick out this fan's particular favorite. They seemed to love anybody who drove. Photos of cars spread across the walls. Trinkets covered the counters: NASCAR keychains, NASCAR money clips, NASCAR fork and spoon sets, NASCAR pocket knives, NASCAR playing cards, NASCAR lip balm. The trailer smelled like the inside of a Waffle House — bacon and coffee and cigarette smoke.

"Sit down anywhere," she told me. My eyes adjusted to the dimmer light inside. She was far from Hispanic. She was thin and redheaded. She'd probably sunburn at the mere thought of going outside. I suspected she might be a little bit anemic, and I had to remind myself I wasn't here to see her. I was here about a baby.

"You speak English," I said and smiled.

"Course I do. I'm English."

"I'm sorry," I said. "I was expecting someone Hispanic."

"And I was expecting a nurse," she said. "My name is Gonzales. Wanda Gonzales. I need somebody to take a look at Ho-el."

"Ho-el?"

"He's in the back bedroom." Wanda left me standing in the NASCAR museum.

I spent the next dozen seconds or so wondering what the name Ho-el could be short for. Maybe he had an attitude. Holy Hell. Ho-el. It was a nickname I had never heard before. She came back holding a redheaded kid with his face buried in her Earnhardt t-shirt. He finally peeked out, and I could see how brown his eyes were. My notes said he was three years old, and this kid looked about that age.

"Here's the card about the shots he's done had," she said, pushing a piece of paper across the little table at my knees. At the sound of the word *shots*, Ho-el burrowed his head deeper into the face of Dale Earnhardt. I read the card to myself. *Joel Gonzales.* J-O-E-L.

"So your husband calls him Ho-el."

"My husband don't call him nothing. Hor-hay don't call, period."

I tried a communication trick I learned in a seminar the county paid for. I paused and didn't say a word. Wanda grew uncomfortable with the lack of talking, just like I hoped.

"He's gone. Been gone. He used to call him Ho-el. That's the Mexican way to say it, I suppose."

"So that's not your husband's car outside?" I looked around for the boyfriend hiding behind a door.

"That's mine. '75 Nova. Stock."

"Well, your car is running, ma'am."

"I can't turn it off," she said.

I went silent again. I was having trouble with this conversation.

"Ho-el broke off the key in the ignition a couple weeks ago. I don't know how to hotwire it, so I just keep putting gas in it. I even changed the oil while it was running once. You try that sometime. I don't know what the hell I'm gonna do if a belt breaks." She was proud of herself. I looked at Ho-el. Three years old and he already had grease under his tiny little fingernails. I saw his future. He would know how to change a water pump before he could read.

"What's wrong with Ho-el?" I leaned forward.

"He's been punk lately." She pushed the red hair away from Ho-el's forehead. He did look pale, but, then again, his momma was almost see-through.

"Punk?"

"Kinda down in the dumps. He ain't happy like he usually is. He's usually all over the place, tearing things up. He's a little stem-winder most of the time. This here ain't the normal everyday Ho-el."

I asked her to let me have a look at him, but Ho-el had a death grip on his momma and Dale Earnhardt. She pried him off like a scared kitten and handed him across the table.

Ho-el weighed next to nothing, like he was filled with warm air. His eyes were big and scared, and because they were opened wide, I could see they oozed more than tears. I managed one quick feel of the glands in his throat, which were about the size of hickory nuts. When I touched an ear, he let out a yell.

"Well, Ho-el's sick," I said.

"No shit," she said, rummaging through the papers on the table for a cigarette lighter.

"I'm going to give you some antibiotic samples. They should be enough to get him well. If you need more, call the Health Department." I pulled a double handful of samples from my bag. "Can he take pills?"

"He'll swallow anything with chocolate on it. Say thank you, Ho-el," she said.

"*Gracias*," he whispered in a raspy little voice.

Ho-el's momma stood up. "I'll give you a ride back into town," she said.

Wanda was making a habit of confusing me. "But I drove my car."

"Yeah, but you ain't got but a couple of wheels left on it." Outside, the Valiant listed awkwardly to the left like a wounded animal. I hadn't heard a sound when my wheels were stolen. I'd been so intent on Ho-el and his momma.

For a second, I found it difficult to breathe. I completely forgot about a child being in the room. "Goddamn chicken workers," I said. It was at that point that Ho-el's momma clipped my jaw with the quickest right cross I'd ever made contact with. I was too impressed with the way she cut her punch to be angry. I smacked the table to keep my balance.

"You watch that mouth of yours," she said. "I don't care if you are from the county, that's not nice."

The dog under the step must have heard the commotion. He came running from the back of the trailer, where I suppose he had a doggie door, a tiny doggie door because he was a Chihuahua no bigger than an average-sized ham. He headed toward me, and his growl made him seem exponentially larger. He must have picked up that whole sound-bigger-than-you-really-are routine from having to defend himself against the larger mongrels and curs of the world.

"Surprises me that someone like you would say things about folks like that," she said. Maybe she thought the fact I was a male nurse automatically put a bullseye on my back for abuse, that I was oppressed. Whatever she meant, I didn't care because I was watching her dog try and make his way toward me. It appeared he couldn't run in a straight line. To go from point A to B, he spun in little circles, one right after another, like a little shorthaired cyclone.

"Your dog can't walk a straight line," I said, feeling fortunate that my jaw still worked. Being a nurse, I knew what a pain in the ass a broken jaw could be.

"Hor-hay hit him in the head with a golf club one afternoon, and he's been turning circles ever since. It takes him a half-hour to get from one end of the yard to the other. Mostly, he sleeps under the trailer. He's not a bad watchdog." She thought about that for a second. "Until he has to chase something," she added. "Hey, you want to buy anything before you go?" She waved her arm over the room. It was at that moment I noticed each item in this particular NASCAR shrine had a tiny price tag.

"Oh, I see. You sell things."

She said, "I got to make ends meet somehow. Hor-hay got tired of wading through chicken guts and left us to go back to Juarez. He said he'd send us money. Ain't that some shit? Going back to Mexico to make money. Let's just say, I ain't holding my breath for the mailman to deliver a shoebox full of damn *pesos*, so I buy all this stuff from a guy in a step-van, double the price, and sell it to the neighbors. Listen bud, Mexicans love car racing. Good god, if there was a Mexican driving at Daytona, they couldn't sell enough tickets. I make more farting around doing this than Hor-hay ever brought home taking feathers off hens."

At the mention of Hor-hay, I thought I saw little Ho-el tear up. Then, he sneezed and I knew the watery eyes were because of his cold or his allergies or whatever sort of ailment he had in his head and throat.

"I'll just walk. It isn't that far," I said. "He doesn't need to be going out. I'll send somebody to tow the car tomorrow. Just don't let them take anything else off it, okay?" The dog had finally made his way to me and was trying to figure out if my shoe — size fourteen — was worth humping on. He turned a few circles around my leg, then left me alone, not agreeing with my smell or my attitude. Little Ho-el was already asleep on the couch, whistling through his half-clogged nose.

"I might be able to get your wheels back. I think I know who it is that's got them," she offered. I handed her my card just in case.

I checked the Valiant. The spare was still in the trunk, so I was only one wheel short. I started along the railroad tracks in the direction of the Victoria Chicken Plant, checking my watch to make sure a shift change wasn't about to come marching in my direction. As it turned out, I was the only one walking the rails that hour. The smell from the plant gave me a headache, and I wondered if maybe little Ho-el was allergic to chicken fumes when the wind blew in the wrong direction.

***

I do not believe in fate. I do not believe in love or faith. I do not believe in any of life's abstractions. Which is why I do not believe there was any hidden meaning in the fact I happened to return to Ho-el's trailer the next morning, a Saturday morning, at precisely ten o'clock. I wasn't attracted to the trailer like a homing pigeon. I was not relishing another encounter with the sidewinder dog. I simply wanted my damn car back. I hated being without transportation and at the mercy of my sore feet.

I took a taxicab back to Camelot. Along with me, I carried a used rim and tire I bought for twenty-five bucks. When I pulled up to the trailer, I immediately knew that things were different. For one, the Nova was sitting quiet. For another, the Valiant was gone. And that little hurricane of a dog was sleeping on the top step, not hiding beneath it. He didn't twitch a muscle when I climbed the steps. I thought he was dead for a second. He moved slightly when the cab pulled away.

Nobody answered my knock on the door, which opened easily when I pushed on it. The little dog cocked open one eye and sighed, like he already knew it wasn't worth going in. I hadn't walked three steps across the room when I heard an entire fleet of cars screeching up in the yard — three sheriff's department cruisers with the lights flashing and the headlights blinking. No sirens. The ten o'clock sneak attack.

"You in there, come on out, right now," a man called through a bullhorn, his voice amplified and cracking a little like he was nervous.

I walked onto the top step, forgetting about the dog, which I nudged in the ribs purely by accident. He growled at me, and I don't blame him. Deputies crouched behind open car doors.

"Sir, you aren't from around here." His surprise was amplified by the bullhorn.

"I'm from the Health Department," I said, reaching into my pocket for my official ID card. I thought it might work like a badge, making us brothers-in-public-service or some such.

"Whoa now, watch that hand there, chief," he said. The men hiding behind their police cruisers all flinched a bit.

"I'm a nurse with the Health Department. I'm trying to find my car. I saw a sick little boy right here yesterday." He walked toward me. A good sign. He quit using the bullhorn.

"A nurse? You shitting me. You know anything about counterfeit NASCAR paraphernalia?" he asked me.

"Counterfeit?" I asked back, ignoring his high-pitched reaction to my being a nurse.

"Bet your ass."

"Counterfeit how? How do you know?" I said.

He raised one eyebrow. "I get paid to know, buddy," he said, nodding, drawing me into some kind of awkward confidence with him.

It took him and his deputies about half an hour to scrape all the NASCAR things into boxes and load them into the back of a couple of patrol cars. They could have gone faster if they hadn't stopped to admire all of the different trinkets. I started to tell them I thought my car was stolen, but I wasn't really sure that was the case. It could have been just borrowed. It struck me that I was protecting Ho-el's momma for a reason I couldn't quite put my finger on. Running a counterfeit NASCAR ring out of a trailer — that was impressive. Her frailness was a disguise, I thought. That was impressive, too.

"Listen, you want to do me a favor? You hear from this guy, you let us know. We can't have him selling fake NASCAR stuff, even if it is to other Mexicans," he told me.

So he didn't know about Ho-el's momma. They obviously thought it was Hor-hay doing the selling. I let out some breath, realizing that she wasn't going to be arrested. The relief surprised me.

I told him I'd keep an eye out, and suddenly, it was just me and the dog and the trailer. With the merchandise gone, an echoing emptiness filled the rooms. "I suppose I'm walking again," I said to the dog, and he must have been bilingual because he followed on my heels, whirling his tiny dervishes between the railroad tracks. I had to go slow, what with the dog and the tire I was rolling along. I was beginning to feel stupid and careless, and those feelings never lead anywhere good.

***

That night, in my tiny rental house, I evaluated what I had and what I didn't. I didn't have a car at the moment. That situation needed a solution immediately. I was intelligent enough to know I should call that sheriff and report it stolen. But there were holes in my intel. And a call to the sheriff might implicate Ho-el and his mother in some way. There you go again, acting like a nurse, I thought, taking care of people you don't really know. I had a spare tire on my kitchen table. I had a dizzy Chihuahua on my kitchen floor. I had been feeding him boiled peanuts all afternoon, and he'd become exceedingly gassy. I'd shell a handful of the soggy peanuts, he'd eat them, raise himself up, then turn a couple of circles and leave a vapor trail behind him, which, of course, he kept spinning into. You wouldn't automatically assume something so small could conjure up an odor so foul. I began to feel sorry for a creature that kept revolving in his own biological functions.

We both fell asleep just after dark, me upright in the kitchen chair and the Chihuahua wrapped around as much of my feet as he could cover. The machine gun blasts of a straight-piped exhaust in my driveway woke us both. The dog growled at the noise. I felt him rumble against my leg. For a little dog, he was impressive. Outside, two men ran away in the darkness, their footsteps slapping the pavement. What they left behind was my Valiant, but it wasn't the same. It had been modified. It was jacked up in the back. Strips of white shag carpet ringed every window. A Virgin Mary dangled from the mirror. A note fluttered under the windshield wiper. It said: *I told them to fix up your car or I would turn them in.* The meaning of "fix up" must have been lost in translation. But Wanda was looking out for me and my Valiant. It had been a long time since someone had done that.

That night, the dog and I rode out to Camelot in the loud, renovated Valiant. When we got there, the windows in the trailer were dark and someone had removed the front door. The dog refused to get out of the car, as if to say that he wasn't interested in making a dramatic reentrance. I stuck my head into the darkness and smelled it right off. Somebody had deliberately made the worst kinds of messes inside, bathroom types of things. It wasn't healthy.

So, I thought, that was that. This trailer was not going to be fit for man or beast for a long time. Life goes on and all that. "Screw them," I said. No more Wanda, no more Ho-el. I said it, but my heart wasn't really in it.

Inside the Valiant, the dog raised his head at me. "I'm gonna call you Roundabout," I said, and I turned the key, blowing smoke and making noise enough to wake the dead.

***

But it wasn't the end of things. A couple of months later, I pulled up to the Health Department in the same old Valiant. I had tried to sell it, but nobody wanted to pay my firm asking price. No one seemed to want a car that looked a Disney ride reject. It took me awhile, but I finally realized the reason I wouldn't budge on the price was, I really wanted to keep the Valiant. I had grown accustomed to the bark of the pipes and the clouds of exhaust that barely disguised the glares from folks at stoplights. I didn't care. I had a loud car that cranked every time I turned the key and a dog curled on the front seat that liked Motown. Roundabout went on all my calls with me, guarding the Valiant. I didn't know dogs liked music, much less did I know that a Chihuahua would enjoy, say, Martha Reeves and the Vandellas.

I left Roundabout on the front seat and walked in to sort through my schedule of patients for the morning. The receptionist, a sleepy-eyed woman who herded the sick all day long from the protection of her desk, told me a man was waiting in the lobby. "He's Hispanic," she whispered like some sort of storm warning.

The man was watching the television blaring in the waiting room, hypnotized, like it was the first time he had ever seen one. When I approached him, he didn't get up from the chair, just kept glancing at the game show on channel twelve.

"*Buenos días*," he said. "You have my dog."

"Excuse me?" I said, which is what I usually say when I'm caught off guard.

"I'm Jorge Gonzales and you have my Chihuahua. Someone saw you in your Plymouth near the plant with Diablo. My dog, Diablo. The devil dog."

"I thought you went back to Mexico," I answered.

"I have returned."

"Well, yes," I said slowly, editing as I spoke. "I have a dog. I'm not sure it's your dog."

"This dog, my dog, is a dog of many spirals. I golfed him once." Hor-hay finally rose. He was small and doughy. His eyes didn't match the rest of him. They were very confident. But his body didn't look like it could back up any kind of threat his eyes laid down. "I thank you very much for taking care of Diablo. I will have him back now."

"I don't have him here," I lied.

Hor-hay began tapping his pockets. "Something to write?" he asked. He left me his address and telephone number. "You can bring him by, yes?"

"I suppose," I answered. "If it's yours, of course."

"Ho-el needs a pet," he said, and, dammit, that ruined it for me. I remembered Ho-el's runny eyes and wheezy cough. A boy like that could use an animal in his life.

"Yeah, I'll bring him," I told him. "This afternoon, after work." Hor-hay nodded and sat back down to finish watching his game show.

***

The address Hor-hay gave me was in another trailer park, not far from Camelot. I snatched up Roundabout and carried him under my arm to the door. He passed a little gas when I squeezed him. Good, I thought. I'd fed him about a quarter pound of boiled peanuts that afternoon for his return to Hor-hay. I wanted him to make a memorable entrance.

The Nova was nowhere to be seen. Instead, an old Monte Carlo sat in the short driveway, its quarter panel rusting, the trunk tied shut with a piece of copper wire. The handmade sign on the front of the trailer said: *Madame Wanda, Palms and Fortunes.* Madame Wanda herself answered my knock.

"Yeah?" she asked through the door.

"Yes, it's me again, from the Health Department. I've got Hor-hay's dog."

She swung the door open with one arm and held her belly with the other. "Well, hey there," she said, glad to see me, it seemed. I couldn't take my eyes off the belly straining against the stripes on her shirt. It took a little breath out of me to see her pregnant. "I haven't called the Health Department about this," she added, patting her stomach. "I will though. I see that in my future."

"You're pregnant."

"Can't slip nothing by you Health Department people, can I?" she said and waved me in. The trailer smelled of incense and sausage.

"Ho-el's doing good," she said. "Let me show you... Ho-el!"

He came running. Funny, I didn't remember him even walking the last time I saw him. He looked as though he'd gained some weight. Color was back in his cheeks, a shade that was beginning to match his hair. "*Sí, mamá?*" he asked, the syllables rolling off his tongue like candy. I don't think he remembered me, but he stayed put, staring like I was an interesting painting.

"I've got your dog, I think," I said to both him and his mother. I secretly gave Roundabout a little hug, hoping for the artillery report of peanut farts. "You read fortunes?"

"Ain't my dog," she replied. "That dog is some bug Hor-hay's got up his rear. Sure, I read fortunes. I have the gift."

"Hor-hay and I spoke this morning."

"See, I already knew that. Hor-hay!" she yelled.

He came from somewhere in the back, dressed the same as that morning. There they were. The entire family, all in one place, almost posing.

"Hey, Diablo, *cómo está?*" Hor-hay called.

Roundabout squirmed a little under my arm but didn't attempt to jump down. I decided to put him on the floor. He began turning circles but didn't move one way or the other. He couldn't decide which direction to aim his spins.

"*Gracias,* ummm . . . *señor?*" Hor-hay said, his voice rising more than it should. I knew that tone. It wasn't the first time I'd heard it, the making-fun-of-the-male-nurse tone. Wanda wouldn't put up with that sort of thing. I remembered that punch of hers in the trailer. She owed me one. I had helped her out. I had helped Ho-el. But the only thing Wanda did was grin, and I knew, right in that second, I was on my own.

"Whatever," I said. I started to go, because that's all I could do, right? I didn't belong there.

Hor-hay said, "So, you are a *nurse,* eh?" Even with my back to them, I could sense him stifling a laugh.

When I turned around, he was in the process of mumbling something to Madame Wanda in Spanish, and she put her hand over her mouth. Hor-hay repeated the same thing to his son, who started giggling with his father. I didn't have my little Spanish card and wasn't familiar enough with the language to know exactly what he was saying, but I had a pretty good idea. Wanda was having trouble keeping her laughter inside. The stripes over her tight belly danced.

"A very *grande* nurse, eh?" he said. "A nurse, but one with *cojones,* eh?"

I must be getting old. I didn't even get pissed. I didn't even think about jacking Hor-hay's jaw about the nurse cracks. I felt tired all of the sudden, tired and lonely. I knew I should just walk toward the door. Let it all go. Just head out.

As I passed Wanda, I said, "Sometime I need to let you tell my fortune, Wanda. Tell me what's going to happen."

"Come by anytime," she said, then sucked down a laugh. "Nurse."

I shook my head. She probably didn't know I could have ratted her out to the NASCAR police. Sometimes people don't know the good things you do for them when they aren't looking.

"*Sí*," Hor-hay echoed, "and when you are here, you can take all our temperature." They laughed together then, like a chorus. Even Ho-el was in on the joke.

I wondered how good Wanda really was at seeing the future. I wondered if she had a sudden, quick vision, if she foresaw me walking by the open window of the Monte Carlo and spotting keys dangling in the ignition. With arms as long as mine, I had no trouble reaching in and starting the engine. Then another quick twist too far the wrong way, and the key snapped off in the ignition. The Monte Carlo skipped and idled, but stayed running. I thought I heard Roundabout bark inside. I slung the half-key and all of its companions as far as I could in the direction of the railroad tracks. I never heard them hit the ground. The key to the Monte Carlo could still be flying for all I know, for all I care.

But of course, I had no clean getaway. When I turned my own key in the Valiant, the engine spun and the straight pipes fired off like an alarm. The fake fur was beginning to sag from the edges of the windows, and I had to fight to shift the gearshift into drive. The tires spun a little in the mud, and I weaved my way through the trailers — no dog on the seat beside me, no fortune teller to predict my future, just me, six feet four inches, two hundred and sixty-five pounds, stuck behind the wheel of a car I had no business driving.

Soap

by Kathryn O'Day

"Can't you just think about the children for one, single minute?"

My friend was red-faced and yelling, his words surprisingly staccato considering the large amounts of alcohol he'd consumed. Disgusted and hurt, I stared at him. Soon after, I left.

The conversation started that night with the usual pleasantries, moving into the more contentious realm of current events around the second bottle of wine. In the past, I'd enjoyed engaging in these exchanges, in considering other views and challenging my own. Tonight, though, was different. Tonight, the political was personal. It was September of 2012, and I, along with approximately 25,000 other Chicago teachers, had gone on strike.

My friend must have known he'd crossed the line when he accused me of not "thinking about the children." He knew me well enough to know that I was a dedicated teacher. He'd listened sympathetically over the years as I described battles with administration over the stupidest things: ordering books that might be "too hard" for my students or offering an AP class to hard-working kids. Once or twice, my friend had volunteered to judge some debate rounds when I was a coach. He didn't stay for all twelve hours of the Saturday tournament, but he had a taste of what my weekends were like.

I'm pretty sure my friend was just blurting, drunk and overcome by the rhetoric of his position. It wasn't as if I'd never heard the accusation before — that in striking teachers were selfishly abandoning their students. It's a cliché that stubbornly resurfaces every time teachers stand up for themselves. I heard it again last winter when parents vented their understandable frustration at the constant squabbling between Chicago Public Schools (CPS) and the Chicago Teachers Union (CTU). In January, teachers voted to stay home and work remotely rather than risk infection from COVID in the rise of the Omicron variant. The mayor, in retaliation, cancelled classes altogether.

I left CPS before COVID hit. I have no idea what it's like to teach in the middle of a pandemic. I have no idea what it's like to teach remotely or to enforce masking in a classroom. Still, I understand why Chicago teachers don't trust the city to protect them or their students from a highly contagious and sometimes deadly disease, despite a stout pledge from the Board of Education in 2020 to stock all school bathrooms with soap.

Soap for everyone. Imagine that.

I wonder how many people who complain about the union have ever actually stepped inside an urban school while it is in session. Sherman, the school where I taught, was so overcrowded that it was near-impossible for me to find a place to work during my planning periods. More than once, I found myself huddled and shivering in the stairwell landing, hands cramping in the cold as I graded papers. Lockers had to be shared, with two students forced to cram books, backpacks, toiletries, and heavy winter coats into impossibly tiny spaces. Offices and utility rooms were repurposed into classrooms with sometimes more than thirty students squeezed in. Space was a constant battle: desk space and board space and closet space, not to mention quiet space. I have no idea how CPS is managing to ensure social distancing in schools like mine. My guess is, minimally.

The school was also filthy, trash cans overflowing with snotty tissues and mouse feces. It was especially bad in the areas reserved for teachers, such as the staff lunchroom where someone found roaches nesting in both the coffee maker and the water dispenser. One year — the year before the roaches — I remember spying an iridescent orb on one of the tables. For a fleeting moment, I thought maybe it was a soap-bubble that someone had actually wiped down the lunchroom surfaces. But then I realized that the orb was not a bubble but a contact lens that must have dropped from someone's eye. I have no idea how long the lens sat there before my discovery. I can say, though, that more than a month later, it still hadn't budged. The table, on the other hand, had grown even grimier than before. It was around this time that I started lunching out, regardless of the cost. I considered it an investment in my health.

In October of 2017, my last year teaching in CPS, I caught a terrible virus, despite all the measures I took to remove myself from that germy building. Two weeks in, my temperature — 103 degrees — had still not dropped. Finally, the doctor x-rayed my lungs and found that the virus had turned into full-on pneumonia, and after another week of brutal antibiotics, I hobbled back to work, twenty pounds lighter than before.

That spring, I resigned, moving my family to a nearby suburb, where my children attend the local public school, which is clean and spacious, bathrooms stocked with soap. Teachers don't strike here. They don't have to.

Some people may view my move as the cop-out of a privileged white person, even though the cost of living is cheaper where I now live and the school far more ethnically diverse than many in the city. Others may think I'm betraying my former colleagues by giving up on Chicago schools. Perhaps they're right. Leaving was a privilege. That said, when I left CPS, soap was a privilege. Does this mean that I shouldn't wash my hands?

The fact is, both children and teachers deserve access to soap. They deserve to feel safe in their school buildings. They deserve peaceful spaces and abundant supplies. They deserve nurses and social workers and computers and books and AP classes. They deserve it all, regardless of where they live or how privileged they are.

Grateful Criss-Cross

by Chime Lama

I'm grateful for the rain and the life it brings. I'm grateful for the rain and the growth it supports. Grateful for the earth and the growth it supports.

Grateful for the earth and the growth it supports. Grateful for the earth and the life it brings. I'm grateful for the rain and the life it brings. I'm grateful

I'm grateful for blankets to be lost within. I'm grateful for blankets to be lost within. I'm grateful to be completely naked. I'm grateful to be completely naked.

Grateful to be completely naked. I'm grateful to be completely naked. I'm grateful for blankets to be lost within. I'm grateful for blankets to be lost within. I'm grateful for blankets

Grateful to lay, expanding stomachs with my sisters. Grateful to lay, expanding sky turning magenta. Grateful for the aquamarine sky turning magenta.

Grateful for the aquamarine sky turning magenta. Grateful for the aquamarine stomachs with my sisters. Grateful to lay, expanding stomachs with

I'm grateful for leftover food, rehashed to perfection. I'm grateful for leftover dream children, whispering in my ear. Grateful for my daydream childr

Grateful for my daydream children, whispering in my ear. Grateful for my day food, rehashed to perfection. I'm grateful for leftover food, rehashed to

Grass and moss, fern and trees – ever so grateful. Grass and moss, fern and trees. Springs and rivers, lakes too I suppose. Springs and rivers, lakes too I

Springs and rivers, lakes too I suppose. Springs and rivers, lakes too I suppose. ever so grateful. Grass and moss, fern and trees – ever so grateful.

Grateful for fireplaces and the hush they allow. Grateful for fireplaces and the interim before death. I'm grateful for this ephemeral interim be

I'm grateful for this ephemeral interim before death. I'm grateful for this ephemeral hush they allow. Grateful for fireplaces and the hush they allow. Gratefu

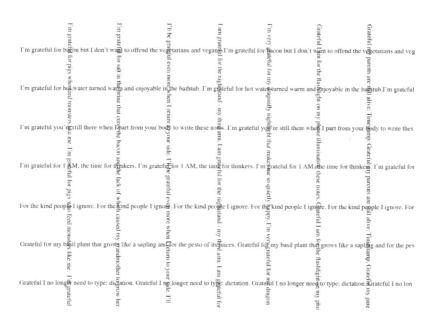

I'm grateful for bacon but I don't want to offend the vegetarians and vegans. I'm grateful for bacon but I don't want to offend the vegetarians and veg

I'm grateful for hot water turned warm and enjoyable in the bathtub. I'm grateful for hot water turned warm and enjoyable in the bathtub. I'm grateful

I'm grateful you're still there when I part from your body to write these notes. I'm grateful you're still there when I part from your body to write thes

I'm grateful for 1 AM, the time for thinkers. I'm grateful for 1 AM, the time for thinkers. I'm grateful for 1 AM, the time for thinkers. I'm grateful for

For the kind people I ignore. For the kind people I ignore. For the kind people I ignore. For the kind people I ignore. For the kind people I ignore. For

Grateful for my basil plant that grows like a sapling and for the pesto of its juices. Grateful for my basil plant that grows like a sapling and for the pes

Grateful I no longer need to type: dictation. Grateful I no longer need to type: dictation. Grateful I no longer need to type: dictation. Grateful I no lon

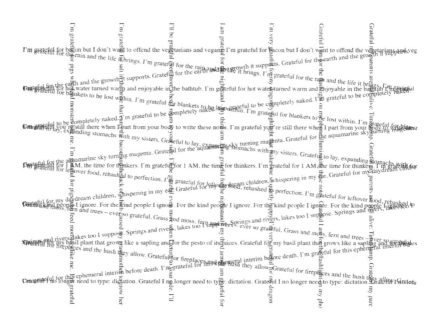

Mosaic

by Leah Rubin-Cadrain

You were embryo #10. You brewed in your petri dish, doubling every day in the low-humming laboratory. I imagined you, exposed under the microscope, and in my mind knitted a cozy snug around your glass.

Every day the doctor had called with news, and I braced myself. Of the 13 eggs that fertilized, 10 zygotes looked promising, and three were touch and go. Seven graduated to blastocysts, rapidly dividing balls of cells, and you were one of those. On day five you were flash frozen at 100 cells big. You looked, and still do, like a bead of glass.

I sent all of you out for biopsy, a key genetic screen. Scientists in bouffant caps probed your DNA for any missing chromosomes or extra ones. Terminal bloopers were common, at 47% odds. They could start from buggy sperm or egg, or live-action mistakes as the whole thing duplicated. Mitosis is a five-step dance with white-knuckle choreography.

It turned out four of my embryos had lost count as they divided, knocked off the beat by a chromosome or two. With these specific quirks, they could never come to term. Two cleared as "normal," their chromosomes sound. And you came back "mosaic."

When I learned this word for you I saw colored glass with light pouring through.

You were mosaic in the sense that some of your cells tested normal, some didn't. You were a mixed bag. A wildcard. It could be the normal cells that would prevail, or it could be the abnormal cells that betrayed your fate. The geneticist typed in written notes: "While most chromosomally abnormal embryos are not viable, mosaicism makes any condition potentially viable in an ongoing pregnancy."

Potential to go either way. Potential that included, she noted: "No implantation, implantation with miscarriage, an ongoing pregnancy affected with a genetic condition, and live birth of an apparently chromosomally-normal and healthy child."

Either way, your room and board was due. The lab reached out: "Keep in mind you have an abnormal embryo remaining in storage. You can decide to keep it and pay the fee or you can dispose of it and we can waive the fee." I'd already paid up for the two "normal" embryos, but rent for you, I'll admit, gave me pause.

Your odds were these: Compared to a "normal" embryo, you carried a 10% lower implantation rate and a 12% higher miscarriage rate. Chances of a live birth were 37%, not even half a chance. I asked myself how lucky I felt, and the answer was mosaic.

My doctor said, "There's an art and a science to these decisions." Art, I learned, is what they call science when it gets emotional.

My oldest friend is the only person I know who does both, a doctor with a studio art degree. And I kept thinking of that time I watched her, long ago, barefoot in pine needles, making a mosaic. On a concrete wall, one by one, she nestled sea-smoothed stones into a bed of white mortar. She followed no pattern that I could see. But gradually, from the light stones emerged a parade of long-legged beasts, and from the dark ones, sky behind them.

The wall belonged to a place in Maine where I spent summertimes, a forest house that smells of butter and wet wood. Where dishes get scrubbed in a dishpan, and beds are built into the walls, like on a ship. It is the type of house that has a towering papier mache giraffe in the living room, without comment. Pottery shaped like fishes. A rope hammock strung indoors and newspapers stashed for kindling.

Mosaic, it's statistically possible that one day I might take you there. We might rock in the hammock like I used to with my dad, while I keep you warm in a striped wool sweater. You might climb the scary ladder to the loft, your sock feet slipping. You might nap in the room with the wall of glass and wake among the pine trees. We might pull smooth rocks from tide pools and sort them, white and gray.

The thing about you was, apart from being mosaic, you were perfect. Your morphology, the shape, the look of you, was rated "good." I felt a foolish pride in you for that. On morphology, even some of your "normal" siblings were only rated "fair." What's more, less than half your cells turned out to be abnormal, which improved your outlook. "In the study," the geneticist typed, "embryos with <50% mosaicism had better outcomes."

The more I said your name, Mosaic, the more I pictured tiles on a shrine in a faraway place. A place that banned idolatry, where artists, rather than depicting God, had learned to tessellate. With dumbfounding complexity, they arranged ceramic fragments into geometrical patterns with, five-, 10-, even 12-fold symmetries. Centuries later, a mathematician would classify these patterns as "quasi-periodic," recurring but unpredictable, hard to measure. Eventually, the same pattern was discovered in strange metal alloys that broke the rules of geometry.

Confounding, renegade, like you. A punk in petri dish detention. Or just too smart for school, running on math a century out from solving.

I pictured this: Your sperm and egg, in spackled smocks, yearning to draw God's face. In you they did, a portrait that defied the rule of law. They stepped back to behold you and fell down on bended knees. Then chastened, scrambled you mosaic so no one else would be tempted to worship you.

You were a backroom deal.

I learned that if I used you, I'd be on my own. My doctor wouldn't thaw you out and put you into me. Mosaics were risky for the clinic's business, a potential blight on their soaring success rate. But the geneticist reassured me that other, less conservative facilities would do it without qualm.

What were these shadow clinics? I pictured a dark alley, a password, a kerchief soaked in chloroform. How would I get you there? A deep freeze picnic cooler? A bike messenger paid in cash, whisking you, in a liquid nitrogen bath, down Wilshire Boulevard?

"Look," the geneticist said, "we've discovered so much about mosaics recently. The study I'm citing just came out last year, and changed our thinking. Outcomes are significantly better than expected. Another year later, what else will we know?"

In the meantime, you kept squatting in your freezer, rent check well past due. I did the research that I could, inside the dictionary. You came from the medieval Latin "musaicum," or "work of the Muses." Medieval mosaics were often dedicated to the Muses, of which there were nine. Muses for everything from music to astronomy to comedy to tragedy. Of all the art forms it's this one, the arrangement of fragments into more than their parts, that takes the Muses' name.

Comedy, tragedy. 100 cells that might tip either way. That might wear velcro sneakers, dirty pink. That might become a kid brother, or neither boy nor girl. You might grow 45 chromosomes, or even 48. Too experimental, in the end, to come to term. Next year's science might rewrite your odds as really very promising. You might wheel across town in a biohazard bin. You might fall from the piano bench and bruise your cheek. You might grow white whiskers on Mars. You might be "good," you might be God. You might stay frozen forever, suspended in time.

They say Mosaic Law came down from God, through Moses on Mount Sinai. Mosaic as "of Moses." God spoke to him, he wrote it down, and those pages became the law. Mosaic Law means "Torah" now, the Bible's first five books. And Torah means "instruction," for every situation under the BCE sun. How should we rule, Mosaic, in a legal case like yours? If I asked you for a sign, would your petri dish catch fire?

Mosaic Law's eccentric sister is called Kabbalah. I traveled once to its epicenter, the ancient city of Tzfat. I remember one steep hill and stone buildings and a pervasive sense of hush. The city is home to mystics, deciphering and divining, working hard to close the gap between the earth and the eternal. By their tradition, our world began as vessels of divine light. When the light broke loose, the vessels shattered, scattering sparks and shards below. It's our lot in this blasted place to pick up all God's wreckage and make things whole again.

I paid your rent, Mosaic.

Who knows? Maybe it's you who'll see where the pieces go. Maybe we'll be walking in the woods, your bare feet sticky with the sap of conifers, and we'll come across some broken bits of clay. We'll bring the pieces home, and I'll get glue, and you'll pick out a wall. You'll place them into patterns like the spots on a giraffe, fitting together randomly yet somehow by design. And when you're done, the late day sun will fix it fast in place. Maybe I'll wet my finger with my tongue, like my mom once did, to wipe dirt off your face. I'll pick you up, cuff your overalls, and help you wash your toes. I'll smooth your hair and sing your song and lay you down to nap. And while you dream of tall giraffes, I'll tell you your first name.

Bloodlines

by Spencer K. M. Brown

ghosts walk under the
canopy of cedars and pines.
everything smells a little bit like
gin and tonics.
      floral and smokey.
      there are ghosts in the shadows
      and I have half the mind to
      speak to them, bum a cigarette.
I lost my ghost in the forest somewhere,
in one of them hollows just over there,
or maybe where the lake ebbs against
the slimy shale and water-smoothed stones
like old lovers.
      lost and still missing.
      but I don't have the heart to be a hunter.
it's a lonely business talking to ghosts.

post-meridian sunlight and whispers
of Aurora Borealis in the summer sky.
we've seen this all before,
in some other life maybe,
one we burned up before we ever knew we had it.
      then again nothing is really
      wasted, nothing quite gone.
the ghosts crowd around the fog
and the forest smells like gin and fire.
my ghost is out there somewhere, and I could follow

the roots like bloodlines.
        white as the soft bone of birch.
        lost in the time it took a
        cigarette to burn to fingers.
but I don't have the heart
to go on looking for it.
not yet.
        no, not just yet.

At the Riverbank, There is a Half-Drowned Body

by Andiver Castellanos

They took you down to the riverbank and told
you God was hiding underneath the water that ran
full of ache. You pressed your aching temples into
the water and a voice that sounded like God told
you to try further deep. Your head swimming
further deep with lost aches. Some
looked like koi fish others looked like feverish eels
the color of moss. Their gaping mouths like open graves
that reminded you of your grandmother before her death.

On the bottom of the river you saw cracked gray
flooring like a barren desert floor. Cracks wide
as whole countries. A muffled voice that
made the river quiver greeted you
asking if you were drowned enough to speak to him.
Your mouth swallowed wet air to answer as the
voice faded into the distance. And from underneath
you saw desperation howling on the surface
reaching down with an iron palm.

//

Your body half-drowned laid on the riverbank. River water ran like rivulets
down your face. Your bones were light but full of noise

//

       noise that followed you since you were a little boy
under a Mexican starry night when the cicadas crooned and your mother
tried holding you with hands that were tired from praying

//

because you had seen death in your head for the first time.

A Final Wave

by Nancy Isaac

The old cassette tapes I find stuffed away in the back of a desk drawer have nothing to do with musical tastes from years ago. They don't feature the Doobie Brothers or Fleetwood Mac. They're 8 mm cassettes from an old camcorder used on many family vacations and I've been meaning, for eons, to get them converted to a newer format so we can reminisce over our kids' younger days. Pretty pictures. But I also know there is a difficult image on one of those tapes. A ghost of sorts from a summer long ago.

We'd gone down to the beach that bright August morning to watch the opening, an event that occurs several times each year at Tisbury Great Pond. At 700 acres, the pond is actually the size of a lake, and is frequently dotted with sailboats, windsurfers, kiteboards and kayaks. It sits on the very southern edge of the island of Martha's Vineyard, just barely separated from the ocean by a narrow strip of sand and dunes known as Quansoo Beach. Periodically, when the level of the pond gets high, a channel is dug across the beach, creating a connection, or opening, that allows water to flow between the ocean and the pond. The influx of salt water sustains the ecosystem of the pond, keeping it healthy for inhabitants such as oysters, white perch, and herring.

From our summer home on one of the pond's coves, we anticipate an opening like kids waiting for cookies to come out of the oven. As the water level rises, rumors start to spread among the riparian owners, those with properties along the pond's edge. Will they open it this week? Maybe Wednesday? Is the level high enough? Binoculars in hand, we scan the beach for the plodding excavator, or listen for its rumbling bass, a distinct counterpoint to the cries of osprey and hum of small motorboats. Its arrival is a starter's gun, commencing a mad dash across the pond, as we sail or kayak or row down to the beach to watch the proceedings.

Everyone who spends time at Quansoo Beach looks forward to an opening because it means playing in the cut — the river that forms between the pond and the ocean after the connection has been made. The cut begins as a relatively narrow channel, maybe thirty feet across on the day it's created. But the churn and pressure of a few days' tides gradually broaden and flatten it, creating a shallow byway that beckons to swimmers of all ages. As you float in the cut, the tides carry you in one direction or the other, like a ride at a water park. The wide sandbar that forms at the mouth is like a protective parent, catching you before you're whisked out to sea. A cut can last for weeks before being closed by high seas or storms. "Is the cut open?" is a question we ask as soon as we arrive at the pond each summer.

But timing is everything when it comes to a cut. A mature cut is benign, a safe place to play. A new cut can be treacherous.

We watched that day as the excavator lifted load after load of sand, piling it to one side of the gully it was creating. I recall our younger son and our vacation nanny climbing up this small mountain to survey the proceedings, then later, well before the digging was finished, crossing back over to the other side of the channel to rejoin our older son, my husband, and me.

The mistake the man made was waiting too long to cross over. When the excavator has just barely completed a link between pond and sea, the flow through a cut is modest, like the runoff in a gutter. Anyone can hop over it. But as the channel grows wider and deeper, the excavator withdraws and the immense force of the pond's pent-up water takes over. It carves away the sides and bottom of the opening, pulling tons of sand along as it gushes into the ocean. Within a few hours, standing waves several feet tall have formed in the fierce current of the cut.

And yet, to someone not familiar with the process, the water on the pond side of the opening still appears flat, almost tranquil. Negotiable. I didn't see it happen, but I can describe what must have occurred. As the man stepped into the water, he discovered too late that the seemingly benign sandy bottom had been turned into quicksand by the flow of water leaving the pond. His weight instantly took him chest deep and the current grabbed hold, dragging him into the cut.

I had been using a camcorder — one of those early models the size of a football — to capture scenes of the opening and our kids playing on the beach. After filming the standing waves, as I brought the camera down from my eye, I was startled and then frightened to see a middle-aged man in the surge of water at the edge of the beach. He struggled to stand, but the torrent was too much, knocking him off his feet and carrying him into the ocean.

There was alarm among the onlookers watching the opening, but not many were present. It's a private beach, always sparsely populated. It has no lifeguards. My husband grew up spending summers on Quansoo and had seen other rare instances where someone was swept out the cut. He'd seen athletic young men launch into the ocean with surfboards to undertake a rescue. But looking away from the sea and down at our sons, ages two and four, he stayed with them on shore. Several people used their cell phones to call 911, but we all knew there could be no speedy arrival of help at this remote stretch of beach.

I raised the camcorder again, not to film but to use its zoom capacity as binoculars. I tried desperately to follow the man's location, straining my one eye on the camcorder's monocular viewer, hoping to catch him bobbing out of the water or his arms rising up in a rhythmic swimming stroke, some sign that he was okay. Soon his head was lost among the rippling waves. I continued to look, but as the minutes passed it was clearly futile. Dread replaced my initial shock.

No one seemed to know who the man was or whether he was a strong swimmer. We waited on the sand, staring at the sea with other questions we might not want answered. No one went swimming. No one built sand castles. Finally, we heard the approaching whir of a bright orange Coast Guard helicopter. It headed straight out from the cut and began to scribe circle after widening circle, its pulsing rotors a sad accompaniment to our vigil.

It took a long time to find the body. He had gone so suddenly from being a man, a teacher (I learned later), a visitor in a swimsuit, to being a body. Instead of leaving the beach in a boat or car, heading home for a shower and dinner, his body was placed in a rescue basket and reeled into the belly of the helicopter as it hovered over the waves.

It was a terribly sad day and I wasn't prepared when it became even more unsettling that evening. While reviewing my filmed clips of the opening, I discovered a haunting image I'd captured unknowingly a split second before lowering my camera. There, in the standing waves of the cut, for just an instant, was a hand reaching skyward. The hand of a person struggling to survive.

A few seconds of videotape and I had become more than a witness, a passive bystander on the beach. I was the unwitting caretaker of an image of this man, still animated, a last sliver in time. It created an oddly intimate connection to a person I never knew, the film a strange heirloom I hadn't asked for and didn't want. I never learned why he was at Quansoo that day or whether he'd visited before. Since his tragic death, the local police supervise all openings and string yellow hazard tape on both sides of a new cut.

Did I neglect that video recording, abandon it in the back of a drawer, because of the man's hand? I don't think so; I'm a lifelong procrastinator of things both large and small. Someday I will get the tape reformatted and watch it again. I will imagine somehow, impossibly, grabbing that hand and pulling the man ashore, kneeling beside him on the soft sand as he splutters and gasps and fills his lungs with air. I will rewind the film five minutes, ten minutes, and he will still be alive. Walking down the beach. Enjoying the sweet salty breeze. He will remain forever braided into the record of an opening, a family vacation, one summer at a favorite beach. The flash of his hand so brief, almost a wave goodbye.

El Rincón de Recuerdo

by Judy Bolton-Fasman

My mother is forever missing from her girlhood.

I no longer have pictures of her as a child or very young woman in Cuba, and so I must swap out the eye of a camera for the eye of memory. Over the years, I have fantasized about hiring a sketch artist — an illustrator who brings victims and perpetrators alike to life in bold charcoal strokes. I need such an artist to draw my description of my mother as a young woman.

I have seen some photographs of my mother as a girl before they drowned in our flooded basement or were deeply buried in the rubble of a chaotic move from our ancestral home in Connecticut. I am jealous of people who have photo albums and family records from which they can piece together a life. But I'm not greedy; I would be happy with a single pristine memory. But I will never stumble on a serendipitous cache of family photos from Cuba in an old attic. I will always long for a stack of pictures to organize for significance rather than chronology.

My mother's connection to Cuba was finally severed when her parents closed the door on 25 years of living on 20 Calle Mercéd. They were only allowed to take a small suitcase between them that held a change of clothes, toothbrushes, and a jumble of memories they could never quite tease apart to comfort themselves in America.

I am thrilled when a cousin in Miami Beach sends me a photocopy of my mother's first-grade class picture. The Xerox travels up the east coast to Boston, and there is my mother, Matilde, staring straight into the camera, seated among other six-year-olds in Havana. The picture was published in the synagogue bulletin of "Temple Moses: Sephardic Congregation of Florida," as part of its *"Rincón de Recuerdo"* — Corner of Memory. For the synagogue, it was simply a snapshot of the first grade class of *El Colegio Theodore Hertzel* (sic), Habana Cuba, in 1941 — a relic of a Jewish Cuba that is no more. But to me that photograph is a piece of my mother's broken psyche.

Chubby and dour, my mother is in the second row seated next to a boy designated as *desconocido* — unknown. It is fitting that my mother is next to this anonymous boy. So much about her life in Cuba is undisclosed, submerged in her fantasies of the Havana she has built up and presented to me over the years. Her actual story is as mysterious as Cuba itself — that jewel of an island whose forbiddenness yet proximity to her, and to me, has always been tantalizingly out of reach. "Ninety miles from the coast of Florida," my mother mutters over and over when she is on one of her emotional jags. Her country has been on almost continuous lockdown for six decades.

In 1941, the world is about to blaze. Pearl Harbor may or may not have happened the day my mother's school picture is snapped. My father, the American Ivy League Naval ensign, is in San Francisco on December 7, 1941, preparing to ship out on a supply vessel that will cruise the Pacific to deliver food and ammunition to battleships. He intuits heat and war and death will soon engulf the world. In 1941, across the chasm of their age difference, it seems impossible that my parents will ever meet — they will remain unknown to one another. It will be the same in their fraught marriage — always desconocido to each other.

My mother will continue to attend *El Colegio Theodore Hertzel* in Havana until it is time for her to enroll at *El Instituto* — Cuba's version of high school. She will graduate from the *Instituto* and lie that she went on to attend the University of Havana. I will not figure out her deception until I am well into motherhood. And I do so only accidentally as her secret leaks out from one of her stories in which the dates of her attendance don't align with *El Revolución* and the years the university was shuttered.

But in that picture from the temple, she is Matilde Alboukrek, a little girl who is aware that she lives in the rundown section of *Habana la Vieja* — the neighborhood of Old Havana that is close to the port. Maybe it is the same port just out of reach for the condemned passengers of the St. Louis in 1939. They are *desconocidos* too — people who perish as part of a numbing statistic; people who are condemned to be stateless and nameless. On that day in Havana's port they are destined to become some of the souls that will disappear among the six million Jews who die in the Holocaust.

History, along with my grandfather, Abuelo, will steal my mother's childhood from her. Abuelo will jumpstart my mother's lifelong crippling anxiety when he tells her that should Hitler come to Cuba, he will not save his children with falsified papers or doctored baptismal records. My mother is a little girl, but she knows that those papers and those drops of water will erase the Jew in her so she can live. Abuelo will refuse her that lifeline. This is the first but not the last time her father is willing to sacrifice his daughter, to extinguish her spirit.

El Colegio Theodore Hertzel is named for the father of Zionism. At the end of the 19th century, Herzl advocated that the Jews needed a permanent homeland to escape the dangers of antisemitism. For Herzl, that place was Palestine. For my mother's family, it was Cuba where they landed from Greece and Turkey in the early 1900s. My mother will never see the Holy Land, once a supreme wish of hers. By the time I can afford to take her, she is hopelessly terrified to take an airplane, and she can barely walk. I dream of hiring one of the many Philippine women who flock to Israel to work as nursing aides for the elderly to care for my mother on that trip that will never happen. I picture this merciful woman pushing my mother over the cobblestone streets of Jerusalem's Old City with alacrity. The destination is the Wailing Wall — bearded with vegetation. At the Wall, I see myself, as in a movie, helping my mother to her feet to breathe in the prayerful air and kiss the holy, wide, chunky blocks of stone. It is the one place on earth I would not begrudge my mother begging God to reverse the injustices in her life.

With the gratitude of a minority who has survived within a minority, my mother tells me that Cuba was friendly to its Jews until Jewish refugees from Europe began arriving on the island after the Second World War in consequential numbers. Aside from resenting the influx of Jews fleeing the Nazis, Havana had its crystalline moments of Jew-hatred. My mother remembers how frightened she was to leave her house on Good Friday. She, one of the alleged killers of the Lord Jesus Christ, was not safe on the streets of Cuba's capital on a sanctified Easter weekend.

***

The blinding white flash of light from another bulky, old-fashioned camera with a hooded photographer behind it goes off, and there is my mother lovely at 12. The physical photograph is lost forever, carried away in the debris and slush of a flooded basement. But I've held the actual snapshot in my hand; the memory of the picture floats against the Milky Way backdrop that always happens when I squeeze my eyes shut. Here's what I want to tell that police sketch artist: Draw my mother as the gypsy girl, or as she called herself a *guajira*. Folds and folds of *tela* — fabric — should engulf her. Abuelo was a fabric salesman; Abuela was a seamstress — a *costurera*. I like that my world makes sense for a minute as the Spanish word *costurera* echoes the English one for costume. My mother wore costumes to conceal her poverty. Abuela, she said, could make the most beautiful dresses from the raggedy remnants of fabric Abuelo brought home.

Abuela must have sewn the gypsy girl outfit — most likely as a Purim
costume; Purim a holiday that revels in concealment. My mother's head
is covered in a kerchief, and she is holding a small conga drum to beat to
music that only she hears. Her lips are a preview of the out-of-this-world-
shade of red lipstick she will wear in a few years. My mother already
resembles the beautiful woman she will grow into. Yet so much hides her
body in the photograph — the brutal modesty her father imposes on her.

On the *Malecón*, Havana's sea wall, my pubescent mother strolls on a
Sunday afternoon with her parents, younger sister, and brother. Her father
insists that she wear stockings and closed shoes; the ocean breezes are a
blessing for covered legs in the afternoon heat. My mother brilliantly skirts
the modesty issue by *meneando el fondillo* — swinging her backside — just
decent enough for her father not to object.

God, how I wish I still had the actual photograph of my mother in the
gypsy costume. She smiles a rare smile on Purim. This is the holiday when
Jews relax into carnival-like, no-consequences joy, and honor Queen
Esther, who rescued her people from certain genocide because of her
luminous beauty, and trembling bravery. Did the Jews of Cuba hope for the
ghost of Queen Esther to bless their sisters and brothers on the St. Louis
when it was desperately docked in Havana's harbor?

Years later, my mother will come in second at a Purim Ball in the
Patronato. Her father did not have the means to donate to the community
coffers and so she was not crowned Queen Esther that night. Instead, my
mother is a Cinderella without the shoe that will slide her into a perfect
happily-ever-after life. On that night, she realizes there will never be a
prince.

But there is one picture I am able to rescue from the ruins of our
Connecticut home — a black and white portrait in which my mother is

no one's runner up. Her wavy hair cascades down her back as she poses towards the future. Her lips are preternaturally dark. She is 19 forever.

Little Matilde Alboukrek in *el primer grado del Colegio Theodore Hertzel*, is still too young to use her wiliness, survival instinct, or beauty to live through the bleakness that her father drinks away his paycheck. Her father hits her mother, and in the corner of their basement apartment — a dark version of the *Rincón de Recuerdo* — he tries to kiss my mother full on the mouth. I know from experience that he will not stop until he succeeds.

I swear that if I had that original photograph of my mother in her gypsy costume, I would be able to suss out the secrets that made her cry, made her hate me, made her love me. At least, that's the fairytale I concoct. I am also haunted by images of epiphanic clarity in which Abuelo sneaks into my mother's bedroom at night. He reeks of alcohol, and it sickens her. He is still wearing his *guyabera* with sweat stains under the armpits as he slides his hand under her thin nightgown.

I can hear my mother scream, *No mas! Enough of these crazy stories! You're a sick girl — enferma en la cabeza*, she will tell me. I am sure she can detect the beats of the machinations I go through to figure out her story just as she heard that imaginary music so long ago. My mother is the one who will be forever heart-sick, soul-sick, and *enferma en la cabeza*.

I can't stop staring at the photocopied picture of this unsmiling little girl who never wants to go home after school. It is a picture of a picture in which my mother, reduced to shades of static grays, sits next to a boy, unnamed and unrecorded for posterity.

When I bring the photocopy to my mother, she squints and says, "I think he sits at my table in the dining room. "*Creo que sí*— Yes, that's him." Perhaps my mother is telegraphing me that here was the prince who would have saved her before he slipped away into some stream of history like the damned souls on the St. Louis.

Of all the nightmare scenarios that my mother conjures for herself in her now gloomy life — *desconocido,* to be unknown, her synonym for misunderstood — is unbearable. *La vida es un sueño.* I hear her sigh these words throughout my childhood. Her life, she fears, is a bad dream in which she will be as forgotten as the boy seated beside her, as forgotten as the man who eats at her table in the nursing home.

After all, who besides me, will care to remember Matilde Alboukrek as the beauty with the dark lipstick? Who will want to help me tease out strands upon strands of her life story? Other than I, who cares if she is no more than a blurry figure in a Xerox of a Xerox?

In my living room, I have started to organize a *Rincón de Recuerdo.* At the center of my memory corner is the photograph of my young, beautiful queen of a mother in a silver frame that I suddenly notice is tarnishing.

Resilience I

by Brandel France de Bravo

Fire is an aria, not a red curtain.
What survived? A filing cabinet,
a pair of diamond earrings, a skillet.

Fire is a contest, not a medal.
What survived? A porcelain sink,
two spoons, a knife, some bricks.

Fire is a sermon, not a pulpit.
What survived? A wedding ring
made of gold, a hacksaw, a wrench.

What's born in fire will not burn.
What survives? The memory of being
undone, re-formed: to *forge* ahead.

Fire is a gasp for breath, not a corpse.
What survived? Seeds of scrub pine,
lodge pole and jack, sleeping beauties.

All waiting for a furnace kiss.

Somatic Code

by Karen Paul

I found myself falling a lot the year after my husband died. I worked hard to convince myself that I was well on the road to healing — back at work, my children managing their newfound status as the ones with the dead dad, trying to figure out how to move forward into a life that I hadn't planned but I had thought I had gotten under control.

But my body told a different story.

About a year after he died, I was headed to my youngest son's back-to-school night. I hated attending big gatherings where I was sure to run into people who wanted to give me their condolences. The energy it takes a grieving person to absorb the good will of others is enormous. So I stopped for a glass of wine to fortify myself.

As I walked out of the restaurant to head to the school, I neglected to note a step down. One ankle turned, then the next, and I found myself on the concrete, flat on my back, completely unsure how I got there, but clear that I was unable to stand back up and head down the street.

I called my 16-year-old son, waiting for me back at school where he was eager to show off his teachers and his new girlfriend, and let him know that I would not be able to make it that evening, and by the way, the sky was really pretty when you are flat on the ground.

He raced over, assessed the situation, and, donning the take-charge persona he adopted while he watched and tended to his dying father, stormed into the restaurant to scream about not having a sign warning customers about the step. Then realizing that practicality had to rule the moment, and despite the fact that he had only started learning how to drive two weeks earlier, he lifted me and helped me stumble back to the parking lot, took my car keys and drove us home.

One of the hardest things about watching your children watch a parent die is knowing that the tide has turned too early. They were too young to be taking care of their father. And now, as I hopped back into the house and splayed on the couch, crying quietly so as not to further upset my son, I realized that it was even worse for them to take care of me too. My job was to stay healthy, to provide them with comfort, safety and stability while they got their sea legs back. Instead, I'd been flopping and falling and creating situations for my children to revisit their fear and their pain as they watched me injure myself time and again in the months following their father's death.

It turned out I needed physical therapy to help my ankle heal. I remembered that I had a neighbor who was a physical therapist but whose work was more holistic. That sounded kind and I needed kindness. I called Annie, who agreed to come to my house for our first session, since I still couldn't drive. She brought her table. I assumed she would massage my ankles and ask me to do some leg lifts and we would be done.

Before I even hopped up on the table, Annie wanted to see me stand. She crouched and peered at my ankles, quietly assessing them for maybe three minutes. Then she stood up and looked at me and said, "Your ankles are still in the accident. They are still in trauma. They believe you are still falling. We need to make your body understand that you are no longer falling."

My ankles had muscle memory. I know about muscle memory. When I was on complete bed rest in the hospital for almost two months, pregnant, a physical therapist would come to my room and move my legs for me, as I was not allowed to even sit up straight, let alone get up and move around. Bedpans and wash basins were my domain for seven weeks. The therapist would move my legs in circles, then in an up and down motion. The first time she did it my leg lifted almost straight into the air, startling her. My leg remembered the stretch. That, she told me, was muscle memory. You must have been a dancer, she said. And I shyly nodded, even though it had been almost 20 years since I had taken a regular dance class. But my body remembered.

So I thought I understood what Annie was saying when she said my ankles were still in the trauma. I wriggled my way onto the table, and as expected, Annie began to massage them. It felt unbelievably good. Any human touch did — I had not been touched by another person in a very long time. And as I lay there, thinking this physical therapy would be a happy respite from the rest of my life, Annie started asking me more questions about what my year had been like, the year of my husband's illness and death. I told her a little, trying to keep up a wall between us. Our relationship was all about me and my body — not the year I would rather forget.

Then Annie suggested something. "While I continue to work on your ankles, why don't you try some rapid breathing. Just very rapid breaths, for 10 minutes. I don't know what will happen… maybe nothing. But sometimes, the somatic breathing reveals some truth about your body that is helpful in the healing process."

Muscle memory is one thing. My body revealing some deeply-buried truth is an entirely different layer of connection I wasn't sure I believed. But then I remembered how, many years earlier, I went for an acupuncture session to see if I could get some allergies under control before I tried to get pregnant. My first session was an intake, and the acupuncturist, after listening to my history, had me hop up on the table and lie on my stomach so that she could needle my back for a "toxin release." She assured me that my body would respond, and left me lying for 20 minutes with a number of needles in my back and along the sides of my body.

By the time she returned, the needles had started popping out and I was sweating profusely. My body was doing the cleansing work she had promised. I felt like a turkey in the oven when the thermometer pops out, but I was convinced that something had happened on that table.

On Annie's table I tried what she suggested. I lay back, and as Annie continued to massage my ankles, I started to take very short, shallow breaths. They made me a little dizzy. I kept going. I thought about the breathing exercises that are supposed to help a pregnant woman. I remembered that panting. I kept breathing. My throat felt a little raw. I swallowed. My chest heaved. Each breath was harder to manage. My breasts pushed up against my neck. I kept breathing. I felt lightheaded. Deep breaths. I began to feel transported.

And then, nine minutes in, my body convulsed with sobs. I sat up, my body heavy and heaving. I couldn't catch my breath. I cried. Wracking, full-body sobs emerged from a place so deep, there was no access. My face hurt. My mouth was raw. My nose ran. I heaved and choked and sniffled and couldn't stop the crying. For 30 minutes I sat on Annie's table and wept out the equivalent of every ounce of liquid in my body.

Finally, my chest began to rest from its roller coaster ride, my breathing slowed and I could at last stanch the tears. I looked up at Annie, who returned my gaze with no judgment, only compassion, and said, "And that is your body releasing trauma."

Dr. Bessel Van Der Kolk, in a book that has spent more than 150 weeks in the top 15 spots on the *New York Times* best seller list — *The Body Keeps the Score* — provides a primer on trauma and the mind-body connection: "Traumatized people chronically feel unsafe inside their bodies: The past is alive in the form of gnawing interior discomfort. Their bodies are constantly bombarded by visceral warning signs, and, in an attempt to control these processes, they often become expert at ignoring their gut feelings and in numbing awareness of what is played out inside. They learn to hide from their selves."

Van Der Kolk, whose research and teaching on the human body and its capacity to hold trauma has become a bit of a hero in our Covid-induced moment of collective trauma, believes that modern psychology has done patients an enormous disservice in relying entirely on talk therapy as a way to address and resolve traumatic events. "Trauma victims cannot recover until they become familiar with and befriend the sensations in their bodies. Being frightened means that you live in a body that is always on guard. Angry people live in angry bodies. The bodies of child-abuse victims are tense and defensive until they find a way to relax and feel safe. In order to change, people need to become aware of their sensations and the way that their bodies interact with the world around them. Physical self-awareness is the first step in releasing the tyranny of the past."

In truth, Annie's assertion that my feet were still in the trauma of the fall sounded like snake oil to me. But here's what Van Der Kolk says about that: "Being traumatized means continuing to organize your life as if the trauma were still going on — unchanged and immutable — as every new encounter or event is contaminated by the past."

In other words, the trauma of my husband's year of terminal illness had recorded itself right into my cellular structure. And every time I fell that first year after his death, my body was telling me it was still residing inside.

Trauma impacts my body. It exists as an uncontrollable entity shaping my response to life's stimuli. The day I cried with Annie remains vivid and visceral. And for many months afterwards, in trying to relate the story, my tears would be re-triggered.

This same somatic response infused my body after a car accident I had in that first year after my husband's death. At a dangerous divide in a local highway, I was sideswiped by the driver of a small truck who decided at the last minute that he was in the wrong lane and moved over quickly, sending my car spinning across three lanes of high intensity traffic and into a light pole on the other side. As my car was twisting and I was desperately trying to get it under control and not hit the pole, I could think only of one thing — that my youngest son, sitting next to me, was once again at the scene of something terrible and traumatic involving his parent, only this time, it was his only living parent.

We didn't hit the pole. Rattled, we survived the accident. And after taking a few deep breaths (deep, deep breaths) I turned the car back around on the one-way ramp and headed on our way to our synagogue, where, even though I don't believe in God or prayer, I offered a few quick thank yous to the spirit that saved us.

For the next two years, I had no trouble driving on that highway. I would encounter that dangerous merge and not give much thought to the accident. Then one evening about three years later, I was driving to a friend's house for dinner with my children in the car with me. As we rounded the curve in the road where the merge sits, I could feel my breath catch and my body tense and I could barely get us through the spot and onto the arm of the highway where we would exit. My daughter, nervous that I had suddenly become a terrible driver, asked me what was up. I told her I thought it had to do with the accident three years earlier.

Of course it did. And I spent the next several months talking about it, thinking about it and worrying about driving on that road. Every time I tried to talk about it with a friend I would start to feel breathless and cry. I finally collected my nerves and drove my car around the bend again and was able to get through the point with a deep breath and careful driving. And I have been able to do it ever since.

Anyone who has taken a yoga class knows that the core of the work is conducted through proper breathing exercises. A perfect Downward Dog may be hard to achieve unless you open up your diaphragm and allow your breath to enable you to reach further down than you imagine you can. But your body listens to the breath; it understands its power. Breathing exercises like the one Annie tested on me are often used in healing trauma. Mindful breathing, when you slow down your conscious mind and narrow its focus to nothing but the breath, allows the body to release its memory and bring a sense of calm and completion to the mind. But the mind might not always be ready. At a grief retreat I attended at Kripalu, a well-known yoga and mindfulness center in Western Massachusetts, we returned one day from lunch and were told we would be having a sound bath. We had to lie on the floor while the teacher hit a gong — a disc-like percussion instrument — with a mallet. We were invited to passively soak up the mindfulness benefits of the sound for the next 45 minutes. Sound baths are ancient rituals, with proven impact on healing and trauma. But not for this girl. Within two minutes of lying still listening to the gong my head was about to explode and I felt nauseated. I leapt up, gave a quick apology to the group leader and fled. In fact, I left the retreat altogether. A gong bath, whatever its positive intent, had crunched against something inside my body that needed to shake it off immediately. Sometimes our breath is just not ready to be released.

I wound up having other falls in my early days of widowhood. But there are fewer now, several years later. I'm also older, a little more careful physically, aware that a small misstep can turn into months of medical intervention and challenges. My body has done some work to right itself, feeling stronger and more capable. My brain has too — I've made a lot of changes in my life that have required deep breaths. I have worked to overcome the damage the grief wants to inflict. "Come with me," it whispers. "I will remind you of the pain in so many ways." But I refuse to succumb. I let the grief reside next to the will to move forward instead of allowing it to subsume my desire to live a more balanced life, both physically and emotionally.

My body has been sending me messages all my life. Learning to decode those messages, to use them to understand my experience, has been a process that weaves both adverse childhood experiences and adult trauma. The physical manifestation of all of my losses creates moments when I feel my sorrow make its way up through my muscles, snake through my blood and my sinew, and cause my pain to double in size and impact. As Van Der Kolk reminds us, our minds and our bodies converge in the healing of traumatic experience. Our bodies, indeed, keep the score.

Baking Weather

by Mary Elizabeth Birnbaum

The trick to flouring the bench
when rolling out dough or kneading:
A palm twist, and a breath
of skillful gauze
keeps raw dough pliant,
peeling clean from smooth wood,
silky to the hand.

The same craft releases tiny, even
flakes of snow on every surface.
A layer between flesh
and pull of earth.
In twilight, thorns of cold air,
the dust of ice, disguise
the planet's deep magma.

Summer will soon raise and ripen
the loaf, the adventure.
Rain will glaze the urban crust.
Patience tunes the gaze.
When you flex aching hands,
shake out your shoulders,
stars sift from the densest clouds.

Swimming Lessons

by Kim Steutermann Rogers

I'm standing atop a diving board, my hand firmly clamped on a metal railing. The water's surface sparkles in the late afternoon sun. My two brothers have already completed tasks for their swim patch — holding their breath underwater, swimming from end to end, jumping off the diving board at our neighborhood pool in suburban Chicago — and disappeared inside the low-slung concrete block building to retrieve towels and shoes from numbered wire baskets. I'm the only shivering swim student left.

Our instructor, a young man in a red Speedo not much older than my brothers, stands beside my mother. His lips move, but the buzzing in my ears drowns out anything he's saying. Mom's wearing her frilly green swim cap. Her fear of water is the reason we're here. My fear is disappointing her.

But my fear is too strong to make the leap, and, after staring at the water from my spot on the wobbling board, I turn around and climb back down.

"It's okay, Kimmy," Mom says. "Maybe next time."

She drives us home in the family car, a 1960s-era Chevrolet Impala. I am six, the youngest child, the only girl, the only one to fail swimming class.

***

I'm sitting in the open bow of my uncle's runabout boat, the sun warming my body while the bright, earthy scent of lake water rises off the surface. Maple and dogwood trees embrace the shoreline. My two tow-headed cousins waterski, swishing and swooshing from one side of the lake to the other, their taut bodies knitting together happy memories of childhood.

We have a pact, my mom and me, a condition on which my summer rests. I can spend my school vacation with my cousins at Lake of the Ozarks in Missouri, but because I still don't know how to swim, she warns, I'm not allowed in the water, and that's fine because the lake is dark with whiskery catfish and snakes as thick as ropes that could swim between my legs. But there's something about the water. I love how the surface goes smooth as butter at the end of the day.

My aunt is younger than my mom with a halo of blonde hair and a radiant smile. "I won't tell," she swears, and I stretch onto an inflatable raft. I'm 13, exploring my boundaries, shedding inherited fears.

***

I'm swimming, sorta, with Diana Nyad as my instructor. The famous swimmer speaks at a conference in the morning and gives lessons in the afternoon. Freckle-faced, Diana stands with confidence and tells me to think of my body rotating around a rod running down my spine, and I swim — face-in-the-water-breathing-every-other-stroke swim. But my hand grabs the side after every length of the pool.

Diana was the first person to swim from Cuba to Florida without a shark cage or fins, a rough-water crossing of 110 miles. She did it in 53 hours. She did it at the age of 64. She did it after four failed attempts. Diana stands on the side of the pool, hands on her hips, "Find a way," she says in a deep confident voice.

At 32, I sign up for my first triathlon.

Days before the triathlon, I drive to a local community pool. I swim a lap. Stop. Swim another lap. Stop. Swim. Stop. Swim. Stop. I think about Diana. I swim a lap, turn, push off the wall for a second lap. Swim two laps. Three laps. Four. In one day, I go from swimming a single lap to three dozen consecutive laps without stopping. There's a random phone on the wall, and, dripping wet, I call my best friend to share the news, the scent of chlorine my reward. "I can swim," I say.

***

I'm bobbing in the Atlantic Ocean off Eleuthera, an island in the Bahamas, carrying a scuba tank on my back and breathing like a rabbit — in-out-in-out-in-out-in-out-in-out. It's near sunset or "feeding time," according to my scuba instructor. An ex-Navy SEAL with thick shoulders, Chris says, "Lead with the mind, and the body will follow," and so I match my rapid-fire breathing with his words and create a mantra: *I am strong. I am fearless. I can do this.* My hand lets go of the boat, and we descend into another world.

At 45 feet below the surface, we settle on a sandy patch. Chris forms a circle with his thumb and index finger. *Are you okay?*, he asks, and I mirror his gesture. Yes. He points toward the open sea. I line up the needle on the compass strapped to my wrist and head out at 270 degrees, counting fin kicks. Fifty gets us to a wall that drops into a velvety blue, like outer space, and my breath starts skipping again until I notice the staghorn and star corals, the angelfish and tangs swimming a ballet around us.

Scuba diving technically isn't swimming, but it is something my six-year-old self could never have imagined. I'm not sure what keeps me coming back to the water. It certainly wasn't my mom's disappointment in my swimming failure. She never shamed or scolded me. For me, water is something more than hydration. Water calls to my being time and again, and I respond.

Chris signals to head back. Orienting my compass, I lead, counting fin kicks. At 20, a shadowy figure emerges. Slowly, the visage grows larger. A shark? No, it's a turtle. We watch as it passes and 30 more fin kicks, we're back at our starting point, the smile on my face breaking my mask's seal, allowing water to seep inside. I'm hovering over the seafloor, breathing comfortably, my relationship with water growing stronger.

We break the surface and the sun, a perfectly round cantaloupe melon, perches on the horizon of slick, calm turquoise water. I take three breaths of Earth air and watch as the orb slips below the horizon.

"Congratulations," Chris says. "You're certified."

The Nganga Solution

by Spencer Harrington

The army helicopter lands in a clearing about 300 meters from the clinic, its rotors slowing to a halt. Three men emerge from its hatch looking as if they've landed on Mars, wearing hazmat suits with surgical masks and clear plastic visors protecting their faces. They hop out and look around warily.

"Took the bastards a week to get here," mutters Kasongo. We're standing at the clinic's entrance and, as its director, he's summoned the men to survey our patients, who now number more than 200.

The men step carefully to avoid the numerous puddles blocking their path to the clinic. It's September and still the rainy season in our part of the Congo. One of them, a white man, sees Kasongo and waves.

"Who are they?" I ask.

Dr. Albert Kasongo drags hard on his cigarette. He's 50, a short, wiry man with frown lines I've watched deepen in the weeks since the first pirogues showed up with dying people. They've come at us from both directions along the Congo, east from Lisala and west from Bumba, horrible ships of fools coughing bloody mucus.

"The mondélé (white man) is Varnus from World Health," he explains. "Behind him is Professeur Ngoy from the École de Santé Publique and following him is that idiot Banza from the Ministry of Health."

The men approach us then stop, standing outside the clinic at a distance. Kasongo and I put on masks, but we've mostly given up wearing them except around patients to stay in costume.

We all bow and wave greetings at each other. Professeur Ngoy recognizes me since I studied at his school in Kinshasa.

"You're surrounded by illness but look well, Nurse Véronique," he exclaims. His Kinshasa Lingala is accented like mine, a foreign sound in this northern region.

"Messieurs," Kasongo begins in French. "Thank you for coming. What you're going to see looks like tuberculosis. We first treated it with Rifadin until we ran out, but the drug didn't seem to work. This disease spreads much faster than TB and is killing three in four people. Inside the clinic you'll meet the few patients who are recovering; outside lying on blankets are the majority who are dying. As you know we're a first aid clinic. We set broken arms and treat malaria. We can't manage a new disease outbreak."

Kasongo stops speaking and motions for the men to enter the clinic. He leads them around the building and outside for 30 minutes. The three men remain bunched together, observing the sick at a distance. Our patients' coughs originate with a volcanic rumbling deep in their bodies and erupt with a force that's long since broken their abdominal wall. Their eyes bulge as they lie on the ground thrashing about on dusty blankets, drowning on dry land. The men stop to speak with our refugee staff, Soeur Domingos, the lone survivor from a local Carmelite convent, and Père Dubois, a Belgian missionary priest.

I often wonder why our little caretaker group is still alive. Last week the disease killed Nurse Charlotte, my counterpart. The three Carmelite nuns who fled their pesthouse convent with Soeur Domingos are all dead, and Domingos now works as sort of receptionist for us. Père Dubois followed his dying flock to our clinic, and, with a constitution rare for a *mondélé* in equatorial parts, says he's remaining to help the sick with "their transition from this world to the next." Marie our cook died but was replaced by Antoinette, a local villager who escorted her diseased family here and, once they died, stayed because she said she had nowhere else to go.

The three men have seen enough. Kasongo hands Banza a briefcase with patients' blood samples that I spent the morning preparing. He's asking something of Banza and I see the minister shaking his head and backing away toward the helicopter. In a few short moments the three are aloft, and Kasongo remains standing not far from the makeshift helipad. I walk out to join him.

"Jean is sick," he says staring at the disappearing aircraft.

"I'm very sorry to hear that," I say. The teenage boy is his only child.

"I asked Banza to take him on the helicopter. He said no... something about a weight limit. Something about quarantine. The army's even blocked the N6."

Kasongo knows blocking the road to quarantine us is an empty gesture. We're de facto quarantined here when the rains turn the unpaved N6 to mud.

We turn to walk toward the clinic. Kasongo tells me they'll run tests on the blood samples in Kinshasa and Geneva.

"Did they promise relief?"

"Now they've seen our situation we'll get some help eventually," Kasongo sighs. "But I don't think they're sending anyone before they look at the blood."

"And they know we have no medication?"

Kasongo nods. We have perhaps a two days' ration of grape cough syrup from a truck that somehow made it through on the N6 shortly after the sick started arriving. I spoon it out in five milliliter doses because it's the only thing I have to give them. The patients are relieved to see me dispensing medicine in my white lab coat and mask. It's what they expect from a nurse, and, lacking everything else, I'm determined to live up to expectation.

Our refugee staff has also found jobs that reassure patients. Their roles result from personality traits that in other contexts might be judged as defects, but in our unfortunate situation are advantages. Soeur Domingos is a commanding presence, a big-boned Angolan woman with a loud voice and severe, piercing eyes. Her Lingala is awful, her French laced with Portuguese. I can't imagine what she was doing at a Carmelite nunnery in northern Congo, her manner better suited to directing traffic at a Luanda intersection. And indeed, that's what she does here, standing at river's edge in her habit as the north-central Congo basin points its pirogues and barges toward our little landing. It's comforting to patients to be greeted by clergy, even if that clergy member is barking at them in some horrible, garbled patois. And while some might be overwhelmed by the volume of patients and their suffering, Soeur Domingos is unflappable. She processes incoming patients like an earth-bound Saint Peter, taking their temperature, separating them into groups, dividing the dying from the merely sick.

If Soeur Domingos is the gatekeeper to our clinic, Père Dubois is our St. Joseph, a comforting presence for the ill. He too wears clerical costume, his collar the only patch of white in his clothing. Bald with a graying fringe, he kneels next to the sick and mumbles the Our Father in a soothing tone. The dying, while never very demonstrative, welcome his presence. Some no longer have energy to cough and just lie still, staring at the sky, waiting for

Père Dubois' valediction. I'm uncertain whether they understand what he's saying since he's never learned Lingala in ten years of ministering here and our patients' command of French is often shaky. Still, the calm sound of his voice is proving more important than what he's saying.

As for me, I'm insensible. Time has slowed since the plague arrived and the remove I feel from the terrible events around me is likely psychic self-preservation. I arrived here 18 months ago, a newly minted nurse from an educated Kinshasa family, hoping to see a new part of my country and help local people. I also chose this post because I was eager finally to manage on my own. Kasongo gave me and Nurse Charlotte considerable latitude in treating patients, which was necessary since he had to travel to Lisala or Bumba to conduct any business with the Ministry of Health or our suppliers; we have no internet or cellphone service here.

I'm also insensible early the next morning when I hear rumble of our launch's outboard motor. Kasongo uses the clinic's flat bottomed boat to make his frequent trips into town, but this time is different. I see three figures: Kasongo, his wife, and Jean, and the vessel is loaded with their possessions. I run to the landing just as the family is pulling away, and Kasongo casts me a sheepish look. He would have preferred to leave without a farewell party.

"Please take care of the clinic," he shouts over the outboard's rumble. I watch the boat and wave as it becomes smaller and smaller on our enormous, black snake of a river.

I'm alone now.

Well, not quite: Soeur Domingos approaches and asks where the launch has gone.

"Kasongo's taken it, gone to Lisala."

She nods. The boat's now too distant for her to see that Kasongo's fled and there's no sense telling her. That might only weaken her resolve.

Is Kasongo's departure a dereliction of duty? There's no point thinking about this: He's gone now. I don't know what I'll do once our cough syrup runs out.

I walk back to the clinic's kitchen, where I've been rapidly depleting my supply of sour-sweet hard candies. They're my pleasure here. Before the plague I rationed myself to one a day, but now I don't limit myself since the illness could take me anytime. The little ball of candy sits on my tongue, its sweetened tang dissolving all thoughts but the joy of its flavor.

Antoinette walks in as I'm stashing my candy, and for the first time I get a closer look at a pendant she's wearing. It's a miniature version of a triangular mask with heavy lidded eyes and a tightly coiled hairstyle. It's made of ivory that has acquired a yellowish hue with age. She notices me studying it and blushes, putting her hand over it.

"It's pretty. What is it?"

"My *ikhokho.* It protects me. It's why I'm alive."

"Where did you get it?"

"There's a *nganga* near my village. He gave it to me."

She's still blushing but allows me to inspect it.

"You're a woman of science," she continues. "This is nonsense to you. But it's what some people in our villages still believe."

"I know about *ngangas*," I say. "My mother was from the villages and talked about them. I hope the *ikhokho* continues to work."

"It helped me but didn't help my family." She's looking down.

"I'm sorry." I'm uncertain what else to say so I thank her for cooking for us.

The next day I wake to Soeur Domingos's booming voice calling my name. She's standing riverside and when I join her, she points to a barge heading toward us from the direction of Bumba. There must be 120 people on it.

"We don't have enough blankets," she says.

"Tell them to stay on the boat. I'll come with medicine."

I run to the clinic and unlock what remains of the cough syrup. I suit up in my lab coat and mask and rejoin Soeur Domingos, who's bellowing at two sickly men who've rowed up to our dock from the barge.

"These men will take you to the boat," she says, pointing at two skeletons with bulging eyes.

They're coughing spasmodically, but both manage smiles as I struggle to find my balance on their pirogue.

What awaits is a symphony of disease. Even before boarding, I recognize the different stages of this illness by listening to the coughing's timbre. There're the sharp, rat-tat-tat coughs of the newly sick, whose still vigorous bodies are attempting to repulse the invader. Then there're the deeper rumbles of those whose lungs reveal the prolonged and disastrous accommodation of the enemy. And finally, there're the fainter coughs — whispers really — a signal that our foe is finishing with its host and moving elsewhere.

And yet not everyone is sick. When I board, a woman with caged chickens asks me how far it is to Lisala, where she hopes to sell her stock. Two goatherds are playing cards, their animals tethered to a hatch at the barge's center. But many more are doubled over coughing, and I presume it's they who requested the stop at our clinic. I dispense as much medicine as I can, but there are so many patients I need to triage. Those with the whisper coughs no longer need me but Père Dubois, who will soon arrive to lay on hands, murmur the Our Father, and tell them that a place with no suffering awaits. He'll carry them from the boat and once they die, he'll transport the bodies with somber decorum to a trench he's dug in a field next to the N6.

That evening I sleep fitfully. The barge finished our supply of cough syrup, and I don't know what to do next. I'm also aware of something else: The numinous presence of the newly departed souls. Even a secular woman like me can't ignore it. They're here observing and, perhaps, guiding us. Because that evening, tossing in wretched wakefulness, I hit on a plan.

The next morning, I devour some hard candy and await Antoinette in the kitchen, sipping a Nescafé.

When she arrives, I waste no time: "Can you take me to your *nganga*?

She studies me for a moment, puzzled. "Yes... of course. But why?"

"Do you think he could help us with the illness?"

Antoinette puts her hand on her pendant. "Maybe."

"Does he make medicines?"

"Yes, he's an herbalist."

I nod. "Good. Can we go visit him this afternoon after the patients' lunch?"

"I don't know if he's still alive, but we can go see. It's an hour's walk. He's a hermit, but you should still bring some francs to pay him," she advises.

That afternoon we journey east on the N6. The puddles and rainwater-filled potholes are easier to negotiate on foot, but sometimes the route is so flooded we detour into the bush. The way is clear of all vehicles or pedestrians, and the thatched-hut settlements we pass are all empty save for runty dogs who scowl and bark as we pass. At length Antoinette turns onto a pathway that winds its way through a thick forest to a hut situated on the bank of a Congo tributary. It's a picturesque location ideal for solitude and river fishing.

It's at this moment I realize we're not alone because my nose picks up the pungent odor of cannabis.

"You smell that?" I ask.

"Ah yes! This means the *nganga* is alive. Come!"

She grabs my arm and leads me closer to the hut, calling out that she is alive and has come to visit with a nurse from the *engumba* (city).

A thin glassy-eyed man in his sixties appears squinting at the hut's entrance, his hair matted and clothes unkempt. His appearance gives me pause: He looks like a stoned beggarman.

"You haven't visited. No one has visited." His voice is a rasp, and he looks dazed, as if awakened from a dream.

Antoinette explains a plague has struck the region, and that people have fled.

The *nganga* strokes his chin.

"A few men with coughs came to me. One asked for an *ikhokho*, the other for medicinal tea. They were the last people I've seen."

Some force now pushes me forward: "We need your tea. This disease floods the lungs. We need tea that will allow breathing and calm the coughing. Can you help us?"

"I can make something," he says.

I explain we'll need enough tea for 300 people and that we'll likely need more.

His eyes widen. He says he needs time to forage but can deliver the tea tomorrow. He wants payment up front, and I give him all my francs because money now feels valueless.

My coughing starts on the way back to the clinic. It feels like feathers floating in my bronchus, lightly tickling the walls of my upper respiratory system. I know what's happening to me, but at least the realization is less dreadful for being familiar.

Antoinette looks worried but says nothing as we skirt the N6's lacustrine potholes.

Soeur Domingos scolds us when we return. I didn't want to reveal that we were seeing a *nganga*.

"You left me alone with these poor dying people! Where did you go? Why aren't you here giving out medicine?"

Then I cough and her face falls and I witness something awful in the indomitable Carmelite sister: Fear.

"It's going to be ok," I reassure, and she takes a few steps back, looking as if about to faint.

The next day I awaken hungry and devour my remaining sweet and sours. I'm still coughing but feel stronger, and my spirits rise further when the *nganga,* true to his word, arrives with a woven basket full of leaves, twigs, and bark. Antoinette takes him to the kitchen to find a stockpot for him to combine the tea and water. Fifteen minutes later she emerges with a cup filled with murky liquid. I won't administer the tea to my patients before trying it myself, so I brace myself and drink deep. It tastes strongly of Chamomile, and I wait an hour before signaling to Antoinette that she and the *nganga* should prepare pots of the drink. It's soothed my throat and made me sleepy, a good sign.

It's started raining, and I'm helping Père Dubois carry the very sick under the clinic's eaves, while Soeur Domingos scurries to collect their blankets so they remain dry. The clinic is already over capacity, and the dry spaces under the eaves are filling with bodies. Some patients won't escape the rain. I'm soaked and coughing, but my heart fills with gladness when I see the *nganga* ladling the tea into patients' mouths as if a priestly communion. My mind is now at peace and the air free of spirits.

When

by Joshua Jones

What spilled glasses we'll be
when the disaster is over!

What friable underbrush,
what sluggish dust now,

but what tipsy geese, what
soused bathing suits we'll

be when the disaster is over!
And what slack clotheslines too!

What permissive kissers,
resonant whisperers,

and even what wistful spitters
once this is over! What amorous

pachyderms, upbraidable
infants, and rascally figments!

What unflappable pageant
contestants strutting brusquely

over broken heels won't we be
whenever the disaster's

messenger confesses it's over?
What derisible fibbers,

what aisle blockers, and infinite
talkers. What abundant

dunces we can go back to being
again once the disaster's over!

What gregarious locusts
we'll be this summer!

Imagine the clatter of our
sleek and hungry flourishing.

Dead Animals

by Arielle Kaplan

You have no trouble spotting them:
what's left of a fox pancaked to asphalt,
the bunny, upchucked, a frayed braid of guts
where its head was, the rawhide husk of a rat
riddled with holes like a lotus root, one claw
articulated against the trailbed, each nail
a dirt-coated comma. You check on them
every day, brittle carcasses your mind collects
like talismans. The squirrel curled at the foot
of an oak with a beetle for its eye is just a tail
by the next afternoon. You tried to explain it
once, to your mother, how death speaks to you,
seeks you out like a worm shivering on the sidewalk,
and she cried into her appetizer: "Is this a *poet thing?*"
The truth is you inherited it from her, from the way
she said good morning to the decaying deer
threaded through the guardrail on the highway.
The nights she played records and pulled you to her
to dance, you couldn't help imagining her gone—
the way, when you see a boot floating in the gunk
along the edge of a river, you can't help imagining
a body, nose plugged with silt, eyes blank
and bloodless as garlic cloves.

Nature is Healing

by Ashley Trebisacci

"... you have to surrender to the essential wildness of the work."
– Julia Phillips

When I *surrender to the essential wildness* of my yard, it's good for the bees and bad for my reputation as a responsible homeowner. I imagine the neighbors gossiping about how "those girls really let the place go," and yet, the lawn looks strong and healthy and thick green with nutrients, and I find myself reassured that this is how it is supposed to be, curb appeal be damned. I gaze out at it in the morning, soaked through with dew, and congratulate myself: what a fine blanket I've allowed to be woven upon this earth. What a quality home for the creatures that burrow and dig and buzz. Well done, me. Well done, grass.

A few days later, I discover what lurks in the depths, and a flicker of doubt asks if it is tenable to let this wildness sprawl for much longer. Woven tendrils of weeds trap in the damp rain, a breeding ground for bugs of all varieties. Small puffs of flies jump out of the thicket where I step, making it hard to comfortably spend time outside. With every cartwheel I turn, I crunch the sticks I can't see, knotted deep in the brush below the surface.

I resign myself to the fact that I have to cut my lawn eventually. But alongside that, a small comfort: with each summer day that passes, I can allow my leg hair to grow unchecked. What does it matter if I let that get long, watch it whorl into half-hearted curls across my shins? Spreading, but not covering, bluish veins I can follow like mazes from foot to hip. My own personal prairie land of the skin, a private wildness that won't bring shame upon the neighborhood.

Looking closer at my right leg: the white crust of a newly formed scar, from that time I walked into the corner of my in-laws' fireplace. For three days, I bled into neon band aids leftover from my wife's childhood, adhesive hot strips (yes, the box said "hot strips") painting bold swipes across my tibia. Replacing them each morning and night, I pulled fast and hard, tearing out leg hairs that lingered on their still-sticky tabs. It was how my mom used to do it when I was little, too — "it will hurt less if you just rip it off."

Does it hurt each individual blade of grass less if I keep the mower moving at a fast clip, racing stripes up and down the length of the backyard? The end result is the same: freshly shorn expanse, the human equivalent of cleanliness, ironically revealing more dirt patches and burnt ends than the vibrant lawn I began with. Absence of weeds masked as care, what's left behind prickly to the touch.

Where the hot strips once landed on my shin, a small bald patch remains — a smooth thumb-sized region of skin amid the coarse brown swirls. Who's to say which is better: that one spot or the rest, the reluctantly tended or the consciously set free, the careful upholding of an acceptable landscape or the surrender to an overgrown unknown?

About the rest, there's not much to say—

by Peter Grandbois

You raise your hand to shield your eyes
from the mycelian burn of living,
the path of your inarticulate want
running through the field from bed to bath.
You dreamt that you were two people,
and now you're nothing but an empty house,
run-down, ramshackle, not even haunted.
Your mother told you once not to worry,
she said life was like going to the zoo,
but the truth is we're mostly empty space
and whenever you left the house
the folded animals were inside sleeping.
And then there's the accident of being
here, shielding your eyes from morning's
hostile glare. Is it that you can't see
because you don't want to, or because
the face inside your face was left
planted deep in the night's fertile soil?
Lower your hand. Do what you can
to create your city. Feed it. Draw
your line. Dig your posts and fence it in.
It's so easy to lose track of things, and
you're in this shape for such a short time.

Kinship of Smoke and Flow

by Michael Walsh

Give me a forest where wildfires ignite

without conflagration, their fury and heat

no danger. Let the trees burn away

their genders, luminous and charred,

and live in orgy with fire beetles

underneath their bark. I believe

in this smoky community surviving

with their nearest neighbor: the river

running in all the wrong directions,

spiting the poles growing stronger,

dumber every day. I trust in slippery selves,

flexible and swishing, like the fish

in these resistant currents.

Long before we existed, they evolved legs,

lost their faith in feet, returned to streams.

I believe in air igniting the seeds,

water restoring all curious feet

to former fins—a kinship of smoke and flow.

With this sympathy, I wish to exhaust

every endless fire. Waterways, take

and remake our ashes in your deeps.

Contributors

CB Anderson's work is forthcoming or has appeared in *The Iowa Review, Narrative Magazine, North America Review, Fugue,* and *Pleiades,* among others. Her book *Home Now* received honorable mention in the 2020 New York Book Festival, and a collection *River Talk* was a Kirkus Reviews Best Books of 2014. Other awards include the Crazyhorse Fiction Prize and the 2022 Winning Writers Tom Howard prize. She teaches at Boston University and hosts writing workshops throughout the U.S. Visit her at cbanderson. net.

Sarah C. Baldwin is a writer who currently lives in Pawtucket, Rhode Island, having previously lived in Pittsburgh, Paris, and Providence. Her essays have appeared in *Salon, The Rumpus, The Lindenwood Review, Thread/ Stitch, Stonecoast Review,* and in many university magazines.

DeMisty D. Bellinger is the author of the novel *New to Liberty,* and the poetry collections *Peculiar Heritage* and *Rubbing Elbows.* She teaches writing in Massachusetts, where she lives with her husband and twin daughters. You can find her at demistybellinger.com.

Carrie Bennett is the author of the poetry books *Lost Letters and Other Animals, The Land Is a Painted Thing,* and *biography of water.* She holds an MFA in poetry from the Iowa Writers' Workshop and currently teaches writing at Boston University.

Mary Elizabeth Birnbaum was born, raised, and educated in New York City. She has studied poetry at the Joiner Institute in UMass, Boston. Mary's translation of the Haitian poet Felix Morisseau-Leroy has been published in *The Massachusetts Review,* the anthology *Into English* (Graywolf Press), and in *And There Will Be Singing,* An Anthology of International Writing by The Massachusetts Review, 2019 as well. Her work is forthcoming or has recently appeared in *Lake Effect, J-Journal, Spoon River Poetry Review, Soundings East,* and *Barrow Street.*

David Blair is the author of five books of poetry and a collection of essays. His latest book *True Figures: Selected Shorter Poems* and *Prose Poems, 1998-2021* is available from MadHat Press. He teaches poetry in the MFA Writing Program at the University of New Hampshire and lives in Somerville, Massachusetts, with his wife and daughter.

Judy Bolton-Fasman's memoir, *Asylum: A Memoir of Family Secrets* was published by Mandel Vilar Press in Fall of 2021. Her essays and reviews have appeared in major newspapers, literary magazines, and anthologies. She is a two-time Pushcart Prize nominee. She has received fellowships from Hedgebrook, the Virginia Center for Creative Arts, the Vermont Studio Center, and the Mineral School. *El Rincón de Recuerdo* received an honorable mention in *Tiferet*'s 2021 Creative Nonfiction Contest. She is writing a second memoir tentatively titled, *The Book of Matilde.*

Spencer K. M. Brown is a poet and novelist from the foothills of North Carolina, where he lives with his wife and son. Winner of the Penelope Niven Award and the Flying South President's Fiction Prize, his poems and stories have appeared in numerous publications. He is the author of the novels *Move Over Mountain* (2019) and *Hold Fast* (2022), and poetry collection, *Cicada Rex* (2023).

James Burke lives in London, where he writes software and short stories.

Beto Caradepiedra is the son of Panamanian immigrants, an inheritance he explores in his fiction. His stories have appeared in *Callaloo, Northwest Review, Huizache, Pangyrus Lit* and other journals. He is a graduate of the Brooklyn College Creative Writing MFA Program, and is a recipient of a Fine

Arts Work Center Scholars award. Beto resides in New York City and is at work on a collection of short stories and a novel. He can be found online at www.betocaradepiedra.com.

Andiver Castellanos is a poet based in South Los Angeles. He studied English Literature at the University of California, Los Angeles, and then went on to pursue a Master of Social Work from the University of Southern California. He currently works as a social worker with people living with HIV at a clinic. Castellanos has recently decided to submit his poetry to different literary outlets for publication.

Andrea Cohen's most recent poetry collections are *Everything* and *Nightshade,* a new collection, *The Sorrow Apartments*, will be out next year. www.andreacohen.org

Vivian Eyre is the poetry editor for *Crosswinds Poetry Journal.* Her poems have appeared in *The Massachusetts Review, Quiddity, Pangyrus, J Journal, Bellingham Review, The Ashville Poetry Review, The Orchards Journal* among others. Vivian's poetry collection, *Ishmael's Violets* is forthcoming in January 2024 (Kelsay Books). At the Southold Historical Society Museum in NY, she served as guest curator for the Whale House. Vivian lives in Warren, RI with a quirky standard poodle. Follow her on Instagram: @vivianeyrepoet

Brandel France de Bravo is the author of *Provenance* (a Washington Writers Publishing House poetry prize winner) and the chapbook *Mother, Loose* (Accents Publishing, Judge's Choice Award). She is co-author of a parenting book and the editor of a bilingual anthology of contemporary Mexican poetry. Her poems and essays have appeared in *32 Poems, Alaska Quarterly Review, the Cincinnati Review, Conduit, The Georgia Review, Gulf Coast, Poet Lore, the Seneca Review,* and elsewhere.

Allen Gee is the DL Jordan Endowed Professor at Columbus State University, where he also serves as the Director of CSU Press. He is the author of the essay collection *My Chinese America* and is currently at work on the biography of Pulitzer winner James Alan McPherson. His stories and essays have appeared in numerous journals.

Amy Glynn (she/her) is a queer writer, public health researcher, and editor at the literary magazine *Pangyrus*. She writes a monthly newsletter called *Outtakes*, using personal experiences as a springboard to explore larger themes of identity, belonging, and community (sign up here: https://tinyletter.com/ameshee). She holds a B.A. in English Literature and has attended various writing programs including Aspen Summer Words and Pioneer Valley Writers' Workshop year-long manuscript program. She is currently at work revising her first novel.

Scott Gould's books include the novels *Whereabouts* and *The Hammerhead Chronicles*, a story collection, *Strangers to Temptation*, and a memoir, *Things That Crash, Things That Fly*. A new collection of stories, *Idiot Men*, will be published in Fall, 2023 by Vine Leaves Press. In addition to *Pangyrus*, his work has appeared in *Kenyon Review, Black Warrior Review, New Madrid Journal, New Ohio Review, Crazyhorse, Pithead Chapel, Garden & Gun, New Stories from the South*, and others. Gould lives in Sans Souci, S.C.

Serina Gousby is a poet, essayist, calligrapher, and founder of her lifestyle blog, *The Rina Collective*. She is also the Manager of the Boston Writers of Color program at GrubStreet, and holds a BA in English from Suffolk University. This is her first poetry publication. She's performed at the Boston Poetry Marathon, Literary Death Match, and HUBWeek.

Peter Grandbois is the author of fourteen books, including the Snyder prize-winning, *Last Night I Aged a Hundred Years* (Ashland Poetry Press 2021). His poems, stories, and essays have appeared in over one hundred and fifty journals. His plays have been nominated for several New York Innovative Theatre Awards and have been performed in St. Louis, Columbus, Los Angeles, and New York. He is poetry editor at *Boulevard* magazine and teaches at Denison University in Ohio. You can find him at www.petergrandbois.com

Spencer Harrington's fiction has appeared in *The Nonconformist, The Lowestoft Chronicle, Night Picnic,* and *Black Petals.*

Kelly Hevel is an American living and writing in Istanbul, Turkey, a place that challenges and inspires her daily. Her work has appeared in *Hobart* and *Hippocampus Magazine.* She is currently working on her first novel.

Nancy Huggett is a settler descendant who writes, lives, and caregives on the unceded territory of the Algonquin Anishinaabeg people (Ottawa, Canada). Her work has been short-listed for The New Quarterly's Edna Staebler Personal Essay contest, Cutthroat's Barry Lopez creative nonfiction prize, and won the American Literary Review's 2022 CNF award. She is working on a hybrid collection of essays about ambiguous loss and her writing has been published in *Citron Review, Flo., The Forge, Intima, Literary Mama, One Art, Prairie Fire,* and *Rust & Moth.* https://linktr.ee/nancyhuggett Twitter: @nancyhuggett Instagram: nanhug

Nancy Isaac previously published a personal essay in *HerStry.* As an epidemiologist, she published research in many scientific journals, including *JAMA.* Also a former teacher, she continues to tutor English language learners in the Boston area.

Joshua Jones writes poems, essays and book reviews. He teaches English at Grayson College.

Arielle Kaplan is a poet and educator from Philadelphia. She holds an

M.F.A. from Boston University, where she was the recipient of a Robert Pinsky Global Fellowship in Poetry. A member of the editorial team at *AGNI*, she also holds an M.A. in Education and teaches writing in the Boston area. Her poetry has appeared or is forthcoming in *The Adroit Journal, Pangyrus, Under A Warm Green Linden,* and elsewhere.

Chime Lama (འཆི་མེད་ཆོས་སྒྲོན།) is a Tibetan American writer, translator and multi-genre artist based in New York. She holds an MA in Divinity from the University of Chicago and an MFA in Creative Writing from Brooklyn College. She serves as the Poetry Editor of *Yeshe: A Journal of Tibetan Literature, Arts and Humanities.* Her work has been featured in the *Brooklyn Rail, Exposition Review, The Margins, Pangyrus, Street Cake, Volume Poetry* and *Cadernos de Literatura em Tradução,* n. 24 (Notebooks of Literature in Translation), among others. Her poetry collection, *Sphinxlike,* is forthcoming from Finishing Line Press. She teaches Creative Writing at the Rochester Institute of Technology (RIT)

Deborah Leipziger is an author, poet, and advisor on sustainability. Four of her poems have been nominated for a Pushcart Prize. Born in Brazil, Ms. Leipziger is the author of several books on sustainability and human rights. Her poems have been published in eight countries, in such magazines and journals as *Pangyrus, Salamander, Lily Poetry Review,* and *Revista Cardenal.* She is the co-founder of *Soul-Lit,* an on-line poetry magazine. Her new collection of poems, *Story & Bone,* was published in early 2023 by Lily Poetry Review Books. Her chapbook, *Flower Map,* was published by Finishing Line Press. Her work appears in numerous anthologies, including *Tree Lines: 21st Century American Poems.*

Dorothy Shubow Nelson's poems have appeared in: *Carrying the Branch: Poets in Search of Peace; Polis IV; Human Architecture VII; Consequence Magazine; Atelier; Café Review; Sojourner* and elsewhere. Her collection, *The Dream of the Sea* was published in 2008. She leads a Veterans Writing Group in Gloucester MA. and served as editor of *The Inner Voice and The Outer World: Writings by Veterans and Their Families from the Cape Ann Veterans Writing Workshop.*

Kathryn O'Day is pursuing an MFA at Northwestern University and writing a memoir about teaching high school English in Chicago. She reads fiction for *TriQuarterly Magazine.* Her work appears in *Another Chicago Magazine, Pangyrus,* and *Triquarterly,* and is forthcoming in *Prose Online.*

Karen Paul is a writer in Takoma Park, MD, and the principal of Catalyzing Philanthropy, a fundraising and development consultancy. Her essays and short stories have been published in numerous outlets, including the *Washington Post, Lilith Magazine, Boston Globe, San Antonio Review, Modern Loss, Motherwell, Red Wheelbarrow, Times of Israel,* and most recently, the Modern Love column of *The New York Times.* Karen is a graduate of the MFA writing program at Vermont College of Fine Arts and is working on two memoirs about loss.

Jeffrey Perkins received his MFA in poetry from Bennington College. His poems have been published in *Tupelo Quarterly, The Adroit Journal, Memorious, Rhino, The Cortland Review, The Massachusetts Review,* and other journals. His first book of poems, *Kingdom,* was released in 2020 by Spork Press. He lives in North Bennington, Vermont.

Sage Ravenwood is a deaf Cherokee woman residing in upstate NY with her two rescue dogs, Bjarki and Yazhi, and her one-eyed cat Max. She is an outspoken advocate against animal cruelty and domestic violence. Her work can be found in *The Temz Review, Contrary, Literary, Grain, Sundress Press anthology - The Familiar Wild: On Dogs and Poetry, The Rumpus, Lit Quarterly, Massachusetts Review, Savant-Garde, ANMLY (Anomaly), River Mouth Review, Native Skin Lit, Santa Clara Review, The Normal School, UCity Review, Punk Noir, Janus Literary, Jelly Bucket, Colorado Review, Pangyrus,*

PRISM International, 128 Lit, A Gathering of the Tribes, Ponder Review, and more. Her book, '*Everything That Hurt Us Becomes a Ghost*' is forthcoming from Gallaudet University Press Fall 2023.

Diana Renn is the author of a middle grade eco-mystery, *Trouble at Turtle Pond,* and three young adult novels: *Tokyo Heist, Latitude Zero,* and *Blue Voyage.* Diana's essays have appeared in *WBUR's Cognoscenti, Flyway: Journal of Writing and Environment, Publisher's Weekly, Mindful, Writer's Digest,* and elsewhere. She was awarded a Massachusetts Cultural Council grant for a collection of essays she is writing about becoming a neighborhood naturalist. Diana serves as a mentor with Creature Conserve, an organization that connects artists, writers, and scientists working on conservation issues. Visit her online at www.dianarennbooks.com.

Leah Rubin-Cadrain works in tech, developing creative new applications for augmented reality and artificial intelligence. She is also a certified California Naturalist. She writes about the intersection of the digital world and natural landscape, ethical innovation, and queer fertility and motherhood. She lives in Los Angeles with her wife and baby.

Taylor Sprague is a non-binary educator and advocate who writes to change hearts, minds, and systems. Born and raised in North Jersey, Sprague lives nowhere in particular and works for a national non-profit that is driving transformation of the education and workforce development systems. Their Pushchart-nominated essay, *In Defense of Trans Childhood,* is Sprague's first publication, and their visual art has been featured in "*Way Down in the Hole*" by Angela Hattery and Earl Smith.

Kim Steutermann Rogers spent a month in Alaska as a fellow at Storyknife Writers Retreat in 2016 and, again, in 2021. She was recognized for "Notable Travel Writing 2019" in *Best American Travel Writing.* Her science journalism has been published in *National Geographic, Audubon,* and

Smithsonian; and her prose in *Atticus Review, Bending Genres, CHEAP POP, Hippocampus,* and elsewhere. She lives with her husband and 16-year-old dog Lulu in Hawaii. Read more of her work at kimsrogers.com and follow her on social media at @kimsrogers.

Ann Stout is a pediatric ophthalmologist, a member of the Writer's League of Texas, and the Retired Physician Writers Group. Her essays have appeared in *Doximity Op-Med* and *Eat, Darling, Eat,* and as part of the Narrative Medicine Program *Off-Script* at Baylor College of Medicine. She is writing a memoir about experiencing vision loss as an eye doctor and hopes to find and bring healing through her writing, so others will not feel so alone.

Ashley Trebisacci (she/they) is a writer and study abroad advisor based in the Boston area. When they're not meditating on how best to tend to their lawn, she's likely drinking tea, devouring baked goods, and watching women's gymnastics. Find them on Twitter at @ishmish17.

Michael Walsh is the author of *The Dirt Riddles,* which received the Miller Willams Prize and the Thom Gunn Award for Gay Poetry, as well as *Creep Love,* a 2022 finalist for the Lambda Literary Award in Gay Poetry. Most recently Autumn House Press published *Queer Nature,* the first ecoqueer American poetry anthology and a 2023 finalist for the Lambda Literary Award in Anthologies. Living in the Driftless region of southwest Wisconsin, Michael is developing Queer Nature teachings and workshops.

Rebecca Watkins is a Ph.D. candidate in the creative writing program at Florida State University. Rebecca's primary interest is creative non-fiction and she is currently working on her first essay collection. Rebecca's essays draw upon her experiences with dollhouse-making, obsessive thrifting, compulsive apartment rearranging, and wilderness hiking to explore body image, relationships, consumer culture, and gender. Her work has appeared in *Touchstone, Fresh Picked Prose*, and elsewhere. Her essay *Blonde Sugar* was nominated for the *Best of the Net Anthology*. She holds an MA in English from IUPUI and a BS in English Education from Indiana University, Bloomington. Rebecca previously taught high school English in Indianapolis, Indiana. She now resides in Orlando, Florida.

Pamela Wax is the author of *Walking the Labyrinth* (Main Street Rag, 2022) and the forthcoming chapbook, *Starter Mothers* (Finishing Line Press). Her poems have received a Best of the Net nomination and awards from *Crosswinds, Paterson Literary Review, Poets' Billow, Oberon*, and the Robinson Jeffers Tor House. She has been published in literary journals including *Barrow Street, About Place Journal, Tupelo Quarterly, Mudfish, Connecticut River Review, Naugatuck River Review, Pangyrus, Pedestal, Split Rock Review, Sixfold, Solstice,* and *Passengers Journal*. Pam is an ordained rabbi, pastoral counselor, and teacher, who leads on-line workshops, including poetry writing from her home in the Northern Berkshires of Massachusetts, and travels around the country as scholar- or artist-in-residence. Her essays on Judaism, spirituality, and women's issues have also been published broadly.

About Pangyrus

Based in the Boston area, Pangyrus is a community of writers, editors, and creative professionals dedicated to art, ideas, and making culture thrive. Pangyrus is about connection. We bring readers to make unexpected connections across a wide range of ideas, genres, and geographies. We also prioritize the publication of new and unexpected voices.

The name's echo of "papyrus" is deliberate: we engage with political and social issues, but edit for writing that will stand the test of time. Our hybrid publishing model — 2-3 posts per week online and 2 print editions a year — allows us the flexibility to publish topical opinion pieces alongside poetry, essays, comics, reviews, and stories.

We invite you to visit our website at www.pangyrus.com and follow us on Instagram @pangyrus_litmag

Index by Author

Back Cover

CPSIA information can be obtained
at www.ICGtesting.com
Printed in the USA
BVHW080729190423
662488BV00002B/9